If you have a chance to accomplish something that will make things better for people coming behind you, and you don't do that, you are wasting your time on this earth.

—Roberto Clemente

LUPE THROWS LIKE A GIRL

SOFTBALL AND SECOND CHANCES

ANITA PEREZ FERGUSON

Luz Publications

Amazon Categories: Fiction>Coming of Age>Sports>Hispanic

BISAC Codes: Young Adult Fiction / Coming Of Age - YAF011000

BISAC Codes: Fiction / Sports - FIC038000

Editing, design, and distribution by Bublish

Luz Publications
Santa Barbara, CA
https://anitaperezferguson.com

To my husband, Bill, whose partnership means the world to me.

PROLOGUE

1990

When Lupe Lopez's brother, David, reached his sophomore year and began making headlines in the Santa
Barbara sports pages with his pitching for his high school
team, Raul Ramirez, the Latin American recruiter for Major
League Baseball, learned of him and his baseball talent. He
disregarded David despite receiving scouting reports on the
boys in Latin America who showed signs of potential for the
major leagues.

In his capacity as a recruiter, Raul spent most of his time
in Mexico, Central America, and the Caribbean; scouting
young kids like David for sports camps and hoping he could
discover a new slugger for the big league teams. He came
across a star only once in his career, when he encountered a
kid named Roberto Clemente. Why couldn't something like
that happen again?

It was undeniable that Raul had become older and less
swift. However, he still possessed an eye for talented players,
despite the lingering sorrow and lackluster enthusiasm from
Roberto's death in an airplane crash.

His brother-in-law, Daniel Villa, who resided in
Bakersfield, California, was the one who informed him about
this new kid he saw playing for the traveling squad from Santa

Barbara High School. This happened at the same time the ghost of the former all-star player Roberto Clemente appeared to Raul like some kind of saint.

"What are you doing here?" Raul asked Roberto when he spotted him on Christmas Eve in his brother-in-law's living room in Bakersfield. "Am I only imagining, or is this truly you? How can that be?"

"Well, your eyes are not as good as they used to be, old man. It could be that they are tricking you," Roberto said.

"Am I striking out? Dying? Is that why I can see you?" Raul looked around to see whether his brother-in-law was aware of the ghost of Roberto Clemente in his house. "Do you have a message for me?"

"I didn't appear *por nada*. I'm here because of this kid your brother-in-law is telling you about, David Lopez, from Santa Barbara. We need to go see him play." Roberto dipped a finger into the chili Colorado on the holiday table.

"We? You mean you are going to travel with me? I'm not dying?" Raul looked around for a seat to rest his wobbly knees. He had not been feeling quite well for months. His knees were in constant pain, and any quick movement could result in dizziness.

"It's payback time, *viejo*. You discovered me in Puerto Rico and stayed by me for my whole career with Pittsburgh, although neither one of us liked the cold weather. Now it's my chance to stay by your side." Those years hadn't done Raul any good. Roberto was able to understand why he had been tasked with accompanying him home.

"You look the same. No one is going to believe this." Raul shook his head and patted his belly. "I've still got some miles left in me. My next stop is Baja California. They say the Mexican league has some hot prospects, and I'm going to snatch the best rookies away. Just like the old days, heh?"

"So you don't want to stop and see the Lopez kid before you leave the US?" Roberto glanced around the room at Raul's relatives gathered for Christmas Eve. *Noche Buena*, they called it when his own brothers and sisters were alive. They had all died young in different, tragic ways. When he left the islands with Raul for training camp, only a small family was left to say goodbye to. Still, he missed them when he'd played in the US.

"No one is going to pay me to look at that kid. I wish they would. If the league directed half as many resources toward supporting poor Latinos in the US as they do toward recruiting kids in Latin America, a real impact could be made. However, they preferred to sign the most affordable young talents."

The Latino kids in the US served as translators for their family and babysitters for their younger siblings. Many worked evenings and weekends. Some worked with their parents in the fields all summer. The blue-eyed American kids were always the ones who became pitchers and quarterbacks and all-stars.

"Why are you sitting all alone over here?" Raul's brother-in-law, Daniel, approached, holding two shot glasses of tequila. "Let's make a Christmas toast to the next season, brother-in-law. What do you say to that?" Daniel didn't even glance in Roberto's direction.

"You may have to help me to my feet if we make too many more toasts, *compadre*." Apparently, no one could see Roberto except Raul.

"Will you be heading out to Santa Barbara on the day after Christmas?" Daniel tossed his shot of tequila down his throat. Roberto reached out and tapped Raul's glass. It tipped forward before the older man could straighten it up.

"Hey, you do need some help. Let's get some food in you." His brother-in-law observed him unintentionally spill the liquor.

"Alright, yeah, we might consider going to Santa Barbara if you think this kid is good." You know, that's my job." Raul moved a safe distance away from Roberto, not wanting to lose any more tequila.

"You've got quite the job. Somewhere an angel must have smiled on you, brother." Daniel grinned, and Roberto also broke into a smile.

Two days later, Raul and Roberto sat in the bleachers at Santa Barbara High School, watching David Lopez pitch a terrific game. The two local teams drew a crowd of friends and supporters. Many were focused on the young cheerleaders who danced on the sidelines each time their team scored.

"What are your thoughts? He's got a strong arm." Raul was still getting used to the fact that he could talk with Roberto, who was long gone from this earth. But it seemed normal, and he was glad for his company. Raul's road trips had become lonely affairs since his wife, Nola, passed away two years ago. Her cheerful personality had made the scouting journeys more enjoyable. "I think he's like a lot of kids here in the north: he's got great talent, but the system is working against him," Raul said.

"The family is behind him, that's for sure." Roberto shifted on the bleachers and pointed out David's mother and father rooting for their son.

"That's always a confidence boost, but many kids manage to make it despite their family situation." Raul stared at Mrs.

Lopez, who was stunning; her smile reminded him of Nola. "Who is the young girl with them?"

"That's David's little sister, Lupe. It's possible that we may have wasted our time here," Roberto said. His comment caught Raul off guard, as he continued to look at Mrs. Lopez.

"I have no idea about you, but witnessing a woman like that justifies my time." Raul attempted to punch Roberto in the arm, but his fist went straight through the spirit. If the stands hadn't been filled with so much cheering and jostling, others might have noticed that this old man seemed to be talking to himself.

"That woman and the girl are destined to face some real hardship." Roberto knew seeing the future was not always great.

"What do you mean? How can you say that? Will it help if we groom David for the big leagues?" Raul refused to believe that something in the future would erase that lovely smile from Mrs. Lopez's face.

"Her son will not make it through high school." Roberto stood up. "And her husband will not be around much longer. We should have gone to Baja."

"What? How can we help her? I'm glad we came. Take a glance around; it's just the sort of place Nola and I would have liked to retire to." Raul took one more glance at Mr. and Mrs. Lopez and their daughter. This time he made a little wave, and the happy family nodded back to him. "Roberto, can you grant wishes?"

"This team doesn't need me. David's team is going to win this game." Roberto climbed down from the bleachers. He turned to check if Raul was stable on his feet.

"No, I'm serious. If you are here for what I think you are, for my last 'at bats,' you know, as I get old," Raul hesitated to continue. He had a shortness of breath while jumping from the last seat.

"You still have a lot of miles on you, old-timer!" Roberto said with a gentle voice.

"If you are with me when I'm ready to strike out, grant me a wish with her." Raul jutted his chin toward Mrs. Lopez. Is it possible for you to do that for me? Let that angel be the one to walk me to heaven?"

CHAPTER 1

1994

Top of the seventh, two outs and a runner on second. Lupe had a comfortable two-run lead and was more than ready to get this game over with and hit the showers. Already up two strikes on the hitter, she relaxed with both feet on the rubber; the ball tucked firmly in her glove, and smiled ever so slightly as she watched the batter making a show of digging in at the plate. *Who does she think she is?* Lupe thought. *She couldn't handle my fastball and went down swinging the last two times she was up today, and now she thinks she's going to be a hero?* When the batter finally settled in and Lupe was ready for the sign, her catcher, Penny, kept calling for the heat. But Lupe had a better idea.

She disregarded the signal with a shrug and went into her wind-up. From all appearances, another fastball was on its way. But Lupe held back so much on her change-up the ball looked like a big fat full moon floating in toward home. Any third grader could have swatted that pitch toward the outfield fence, but the batter had already finished her swing before the ball even reached the plate and settled softly in Penny's mitt. The ump called out, "Ball game!"

The Lady Dons softball team marked their seventh consecutive victory with a celebration. The girls were on a streak, dancing around in their locker room, waiting to shower. Sneaking a glance through the swinging doors connecting to the gymnasium, a nerdy freshman gawked at the senior players, who were half-naked.

"What do you think you are doing in here?" The team's catcher, Penny, prevented the younger girl from entering while taking a firm stance with her hands on her hips. Both on the field and off, Penny was accustomed to being dominant. The freshman grimaced and moved back.

"Are you the panty police or something? Put on some clothes and let the kid in." Lupe, the team's pitcher, said.

"I have a message from Ms. Granger in the counseling office," the freshman stammered. "It's for Lupe Lopez and Penny Williams."

"Give me that piece of paper." Lupe snatched it from the girl's grasp. From her perspective, high school was a constant stream of problems. She had a lot of pressure from her family to be the first to graduate, secure a scholarship, and play at the university, but the closer she got, the more it seemed like an impossible feat.

"Oh, Luuu-pe, Pen-ney!" Carrie, who played first base, mocked the girls. "Are you in trouble?" As she continued to dance around in her underwear, music blared, and the showers filled the space with steam.

The girl's gym and locker room were the oldest part of the high school sports complex. The tile floors were covered with slick film, and the hot water ran out long before the whole team showered. Rusted lockers cramped the space; their doors banged shut and often jammed. The freshman lost her balance when Lupe grabbed the piece of paper. She skidded back toward the door, and Lupe caught her by the arm to keep her from more embarrassment.

"Goodbye, kid! First dibs!" The players scrambled to get their share of hot water, lathering up with flowery-smelling body wash and shampoos. Carrie discarded half-used bottles of product and did not seem to care about the waste. Lupe reached into the back of her locker to find her remaining bar of Ivory soap. Her teammates discarded fancy bottles that she desperately wanted to retrieve, but she was too fearful. The unread message from Ms. Granger lay under her street clothes. Before Lupe finished her shower, the water turned icy cold.

"What did you do with the piece of paper? Does it apply to both of us?" Penny was already dressed. She rummaged through the locker. Lupe had grown accustomed to her nosy ways and didn't want to upset her trusted friend. They worked as a team, the pitcher and the catcher. Lupe never felt connected to her other teammates. The only place she felt appreciated was when she was on the mound, blowing her fastball past all the hitters. She loved the sport.

"What's this other note, something from your mommy?" Penny read in a sappy voice. "Make us proud."

Lupe's face turned red hot, her mama's voice echoing in her head. "Haznos sentir orgullosos, Lupe—make us proud."

"Come on, stop going through my things." Lupe offered the counselor's note to Penny. "Here, nosy, you read it."

"Is that a notice from Ms. Granger?" Coach Collins came into the locker room. She saw the note being passed. "Let me see it. You two have waited too long to do your community service hours."

"Is that what this is all about?" Lupe could never escape grown-ups who wanted to tell her what to do.

"I'm trying to help you. Community service is required for every graduate. It would be a shame to default on your university player's contract if you couldn't graduate," Coach said.

While getting dressed, Lupe could not shake the words "default on your university contract" from her thoughts. This marked her very first signed contract. Lupe had been excited during her conversation with the recruiter. She hadn't thought about the possibility of not fulfilling her part of the university contract. However, failure was now a genuine and dreadful possibility.

Coach Collin's interruption did not bother Penny at all. She placed the note inside her duffel bag.

"I'm crossing my fingers that our Mrs. Macias can wash away these grass stains." Penny tossed her uniform in the team's laundry hamper. "Just so you know, you made quite the impression on that recruiter when you were pitching today. It was as if you had a giant sign on your jersey that said, 'Watch me.'"

After giving a nod to Coach Collins, Lupe folded her uniform and made a mental note to wash it herself at home after finishing cleaning the kitchen. She eagerly looked forward to the end of their season, the end of the school year, and this summer's sports camp, where she would have a chance to show off her skills.

"We'll both be watched a lot this summer."

"Camp, yeah. Cool." Penny nodded. "Wait, a minute; let me read that note again." She read the note from the counselor aloud. "'My records show that neither of you met the graduation requirement of sixty hours of community service.' Coach Collins is right."

"There's always something. I'm counting down the days until I graduate and escape from here."

"Interested in a lift?" Penny asked. Lupe always managed to find a way to decline, no matter how many times Penny offered. "Let me guess, 'No, not today.' You're so stubborn."

"Hey, I'm in training." Lupe lifted her books wrapped in her hoodie. "I'm working on strengthening my pitching arm. Hasta mañana." Lupe waved off her friend.

She strolled down the street in the opposite direction of Penny, ensuring Penny remained unaware that Lupe's family lived in the tiniest house in a humble neighborhood of rented homes—some well maintained, others deteriorating. When the college recruiter had wanted to talk to Mama at home, Lupe lied, claiming that all recruiting meetings had to occur at school. She assumed every other member of her high school softball team lived in the same way as Penny.

When she got home, Lupe shoved a frozen meal into the microwave and turned on the TV to find the Women's Collegiate Softball Finals. She read the "Live Healthy" meal box: "This delicious meal provides twelve grams of protein for strength and energy while avoiding additional fat and carbohydrates."

When dinner was ready and the first pitch was about to be delivered, Lupe climbed into Papa's favorite chair. He would not be using it. She propped her meal on her lap. The first bite was spicy, but nowhere near as good as Mama's chili. It had been a long time since she had fixed that meal. Dinner was not satisfying without fat and carbohydrates—enchiladas, tortillas, and beans. Mama was at work all the time these days, and David, Lupe's brother, was cruising somewhere in Papa's old Chevy.

Lupe flashed back to the old days when it had been her job to clear the table while Mama worked in the kitchen. David's mitt, nicknamed Roberto, had always cluttered the dinner table, propped on Abuela Alicia's photo. How many times had Mama reminded him to keep it out of the dining room?

"Afuera, outdoors, David," Mama would say.

The TV picture looked fuzzy, and the first inning of the softball finals was lackluster. Lupe thought more about the old days, which were just last year. David had been home; he took time to have a catch with her. Mama never worked through dinner, and Papa had been alive.

During her junior year, Lupe had attempted to join the softball team after being dared by her brother. She did not know anyone on the team. Most of the other girls were debutante types who wore designer jeans. Somehow Lupe and Penny, the catcher, became friends, and now they were both hoping to attend university to play ball after graduation. They joked about being salt and pepper—the tall white girl and the short dark girl.

Lupe unhooked her cleats from her backpack. They were still warm from the afternoon's practice. She tossed them in the corner, where they plopped down in a cloud of dirt. They lay there in contrast to Mama's tidy house, small but clean.

By the time she finished her microwave meal, a mound of tough chopped green vegetables filled one corner of the box. Lupe thought of her Earth studies teacher, Ms. Enviro-Mental, as the students called her. If it were up to her, the entire house would be one big recycling plant.

"Rinse all paper packaging and recycle it, clean all cans and bottles and recycle them. Shred all newspapers, flyers, and programs, and recycle them. Eggshells, food scraps, coffee grounds, banana peels all go into a compost pile. They decompose in sixty days; after that, turn them into compost mulch and recycle them in your organic garden," Ms. Enviro-Mental lectured. She must live in a different world than the

Lopez household, where all foodstuffs became leftovers, all old clothes were altered, all birthday cards were reused, and all vegetable scraps went to Shelly.

CHAPTER 2

Shelly lived in a sandbox in the backyard. Eight years ago, when Lupe was ten, the family had their one and only vacation to Arizona to visit Grandma Lopez in Flagstaff. In Lupe's memory, it was a lot of driving, a lot of desert, and a lot of sitting quietly while the adults spoke Spanish, most of which she didn't even try to understand since they were old, and everything they thought and said was boring. David kept his nose buried in three comic books for the entire seven days. She wasn't sure whether he was a slow reader or reading each one seven times. Her books were different. They were coloring books and kept her occupied in a world of imagination.

Lunch was comprised of what Mama called provisions, from a food box carried from home and opened on the side of a wide road or at a state-sponsored rest stop, where the bathrooms were stinky and the wooden picnic benches had splinters and sticky spots from the last family who'd stopped with peanut butter and jelly sandwiches.

A real fast-food restaurant with indoor seating was never in the budget or in the plans for the Lopez family. But on day seven there was a new experience in store as the golden arches appeared along the highway. Lupe put away her coloring book and prepared herself for a treat. Many other travelers were making the same lunch stop on the same day in the same spot. Lupe could see that they were more experienced with fast-food stops than the Lopez family. Other dads approached the counter with their family's custom order already memorized for the clerk, usually a teenager, who stood opposite the customer and punched a greasy cash register to add up the menu selections, ring a total, and rip off a long paper ribbon receipt. They circled the last line on the tab before handing it to the dads, who were busy fumbling with their wallets and grumbling about cost increases.

"This is your order number." The clerk passed the receipt, took the money, and faced a new dad to say, "May I have your order, please?" There was no way Lupe's papa was prepared for this rapid-fire exchange.

Meanwhile, the mom of the family mopped up their selected table with a little box of wipes they carried in their purse. They even wiped the seats before placing backpacks, jackets, and purses as placeholders to mark the family's territory. The kids worked the soda machine like expert bartenders. Ice clanked into tall plastic glasses; soda selections were organized for the entire family. They squirted condiments like ketchup, relish, and mustard into tiny paper cups and transported them to the family table by the time the circled number on the end of the receipt was called out by the pickup clerk who was surrounded by hungry customers.

In the end, it was Lupe's mama, not Papa, who ordered for the Lopez family. Her English was better. She kept an eagle eye on the cost of each item, summing up the money in her purse and the amount it would take to buy enough gasoline to get home.

"You kids can each get your own hamburger, but you'll have to share an order of french fries and a soda." Lupe hoped the other feasting families could not overhear her mama. "Your papa and I will split a burger. Just put water in a paper cup for us." Lupe could have carried the entire family order on one small tray, but they left that duty to Papa, who seemed proud to parade through the other diners at their reserved tables.

Luckily, only outside tables were available, so Lupe and David could hide their shame of dividing fries and sharing one soda. Mama and Papa did not seem to notice the slim pickings at their table compared with those of the other guests crowded at the inside tables. Mama made a show of wiping up every crumb and smear with a free paper napkin. She shook the paper over a trash can, then smoothed it, folded it, and added it to her purse for later use. Lupe noticed that there was more wasted food in the trash can than her own family had on their entire tray.

After lunch, Papa wandered off to the edge of the parking lot. Lupe watched as he stooped to collect something on the ground. She rushed toward him, curious but embarrassed by his behavior.

"Look, Lupe." Papa held out his hand, palm up. In the middle of his hand lay a small gray circle, a kind of bump like a smooth rock. Then four tiny feet wiggled out from beneath the circle. Lupe thought of her coloring book page with the turtle family. "It's alive. Go ask your mama if you can keep it," Papa said in a whisper.

Mama took out her used napkin to form a little nest for the creature only three inches long. The family, now increased by one tiny beating heart, packed themselves into the car for the ride home.

"I'm going to call her Shelly. A loud, silly girl at school has that name, but this quiet little shell girl is perfect for that name." Lupe stroked the shell as gently as possible.

"You can keep track of her and feed her, so you can name her. Now you will be a mama," Mama said as she winked at Papa. "David, you can build her a home." He pretended to read his comic book, but the corner of his mouth turned up in a smile.

For two weeks after their return from Flagstaff, David and Papa spent every evening making a home for Shelly. In the meantime, she lived in a shoe box, and Lupe learned what she would eat—tiny pieces of vegetables, small bottle caps full of water. During the day, she stayed still. At night, Lupe lit a lamp near her box. By morning, Shelly had moved to a new corner of the box.

After two weeks, they celebrated the grand opening of Shelly's home. Papa and David had made a frame from old wooden pallets recovered from the back of the grocery store and nailed them together. After several trips to the beach, they filled it with sand. It was like a big sandbox for tiny Shelly. That seemed like a long time ago now . . .

"Here we go, supper for the lady in a big box." Lupe took a break from the game on TV and scattered the vegetable scraps from her meal on the sand. "That's dinner; get used to it." Lupe bent down to give Shelly a gentle tap. She was eight inches bigger than the day Papa found her in Arizona. She had grown one inch a year. Lupe intended to come back after the game and turn on the night lamp. "Sometimes things change, and it takes a while to get used to them," Lupe said to Shelly.

Meanwhile, Lisa Fernandez was the best thing about the game on TV. She pitched for UCLA. Lupe squinted at the tiny TV screen to study Lisa's stance on the rubber and her windup. In one spectacular play the batter hit Lisa's pitch into left field, the fielder threw to the shortstop, who threw beyond the catcher, who then had to chase the ball behind the plate. Lisa ran in from the infield to cut the runner off at home. Wham! She was thrown off her feet by the runner but held the ball high in the air after the tag. Out!

"I would do anything if only I could play like that for a college team," Lupe said out loud. "How am I going to make anyone proud, all alone in this shoebox of a house, eating a stupid frozen dinner while my mama works every night? Papa left us penniless, and David already dropped out of school. I've got to get through graduation, that's it."

Santa Barbara Sporting News

A Roll Call from Our Local Teams

Spring 1994

Midseason—Coach Nancy Collins— SBHS Women's Softball

A recent report from SBHS Women's Softball, Coach Nancy Collins, indicates she has high expectations for the final weeks of the season. "Our experienced team performs at its peak, using fundamental skills, excellent cooperation, and a winning spirit."

Coach Collins returned to her alma mater to coach the SBHS Lady Dons in 1989. "We've just set a seven-game winning streak due to the hard work and excellent training by this team. The weeks ahead will be a challenge, but I believe we are ready. The chemistry is really good," she said.

The Dons, now 7–3 at midseason, have already profited from the wisdom of their coach. They take on the Lady Lions next week, Thursday at 2:00 p.m., in Camarillo.

CHAPTER 3

The following morning, with images of Lisa Fernandez still in her mind, Lupe brushed the dirt from her cleats and hung them back on her backpack. Mama would be furious if she saw the shoes were dirty, but that was the way Lupe liked them. It was the way the other girls' shoes looked. Mama valued clean white shoes more than pitching a winning game. Lupe headed back to school and waited for Penny in the student parking lot.

The main building of the high school looked like an old castle. The entrance was decorated with intricate designs and enormous statues. Above the door, a tall tower held a huge bell that was rung after winning games and on special occasions.

Lupe recalled her initial day on campus, scanning for fellow brown faces amid the enthusiastic, laughing students. The school was built on a mesa. Behind it, rolling hills held wealthy homes. Below, the neighborhoods were full of working-class families.

It didn't take Lupe too long to find the other kids who looked like her in the remedial English and math classes or in gym class. But none of the other Mexican girls liked sports or the required gym clothes. In her freshman year, she realized she didn't have much in common with those girls, who chattered about dates, makeup, clothes, and boys. Lupe looked outside their circle and over their shoulders to see the girls who stayed after classes and suited up for practice on the athletic fields. She thought to herself, these girls are strong and independent.

"Penny, we gotta go. Come on." The two girls raced toward the counselor's office. At 8:23, they knocked on Ms. Granger's door.

"Close call, girls." The counselor opened the door. "You are both in big trouble."

"Both of us?" they said together.

"Why haven't you done any community service hours? You know it's required before graduation," Ms. Granger said.

"What? Don't sports count? We don't have time for anything else when we have practice every day." Lupe had a bad feeling about this.

"Sports are good, and if you were coaching little kids, that could count. But just being on the team? I'm afraid not. You are lucky I got a request for volunteers yesterday. The placement will be six hours a week for the last six weeks before graduation," Ms. Granger said.

"But we've got practice. We can't do this." Lupe and Penny let their mouths drop open in disbelief.

"Oh yes, you can. Actually, you have to do it for graduation. It's the law." Ms. Granger was not budging. "You will volunteer on Monday, Wednesday, and Friday, from five to seven in the evening, after practice. It's just down the street— Villa Santa Barbara."

"What's that?" Penny said.

"That's the old people's home—no way!" Lupe knew the place all too well. Her mother did the retirees' laundry on the midnight shift.

"Ugh!" Penny said.

"It's not so bad. You get a free meal," Ms. Granger explained, as if it was something to be excited about. "You just spend one hour eating with the residents and another hour visiting after dinner. It's easy."

"You've got to be kidding." Lupe was mortified. It was bad enough to have to do the hours, but at the same place Mama did the dirty laundry? That was exactly why she wanted to graduate, to do something better with her life.

"What do they eat?" Penny said.

"They have normal food, Penny. And they are waiting for you. Go introduce yourselves tonight. Now get going." Ms. Granger rolled her eyes, as if she had gone out of her way to do something nice and the girls didn't appreciate it.

A young man who was both dark and handsome stepped out of the front door of Villa Santa Barbara as Lupe and Penny were nearing. There was something about him that seemed slightly familiar. Lupe led the way and avoided telling Penny how she knew about the Villa. Most people assumed this building was just another high-dollar hotel in the downtown neighborhood.

"Is this it? Wow! I hope they all look like that guy." Penny was not embarrassed to give the young man the once-over.

"*Chicas.*" The man held the door for the girls and addressed Lupe, who blushed and nodded at him. "*Buenos zapatos,* nice shoes." He admired her cleats hanging from her backpack.

"So hi. I, ah—" Penny tried to start a conversation with the man, but Lupe grabbed her arm and pulled her into the entrance. "Hey! What's the deal, Lupe?"

"Let's just get this over with," Lupe said. Inside, the lobby looked fancy, not sterile, like the hospital setting that they anticipated. The only other part of the building that Lupe had visited was the deep underground parking lot and the laundry room stationed in one corner. Here in the lobby, the rugs, a chandelier, and paintings hanging on the walls were a surprise.

"Sure smells like dinnertime. God, I'm starved." Penny checked out a long mahogany counter in the reception area, and then followed her nose to the dining room. A middle-aged woman intercepted the girls.

"Are you here to visit a resident?" The woman lowered a pair of glasses from the top of her head to examine the girls. Her brown hair was pulled back in a low ponytail. "No, I'll bet you are the girls from the high school—the softball players, right?" The woman wore a long, loose skirt and a pastel blouse with a square plastic badge on her pocket that read, GINNY ROGERS, SALES. "I have some experience playing baseball from my school days."

It was hard to imagine she had ever run the bases. Lupe tried to guess what position she once played. How long ago had it been? Sales? She couldn't think of what she sold here, but it was obvious that this was their contact person.

"Ms. Granger told me all about you. I'm so glad you are going to join us here at the Villa. You'll love the residents. They get so excited to have young people visit." Ginny handed them each a card labeled VSB INFORMATION CARD and asked them to fill in the questions about their addresses and phone numbers. After they scribbled down their information, she resumed a cheery conversation.

"Let's go meet a few folks. Are you hungry?" She spoke like Lupe's kindergarten teacher, almost overly kind. "We're having fried chicken and mashed potatoes tonight."

"Excellent!" Penny was all in and ready to eat. How could she be so enthusiastic? Lupe wondered how she would react when she actually saw the old people. As soon as they entered the dining room, conversations were hushed. Then high-pitched voices called out to them.

"We have seats here, girls. Come join us." Three ladies with blue eyes and puffy silver hair sat on one side of a large round table with a jar of fake flowers in the center. "Are you visiting someone? You look just like my granddaughter." They spoke directly to Penny and ignored Lupe. "Sit down, sit down."

As soon as the girls sat down, a young woman in a white apron who looked a lot like Lupe approached and asked if they would like chicken and potatoes.

"Sure they would," the silver-haired trio answered for them. "And bring them something to drink, too. Tea, juice, milk?" There was no need for Lupe to talk. Everything was brought to her. However, the ladies seemed to be much more interested in becoming acquainted with Penny, peppering her with questions and compliments. There was nothing new about that.

From the next table, Lupe heard a gravelly low voice repeating one word. "*Sal.*" She stole a quick glance, and sure enough, there was a large round man sitting in a wheelchair, all alone at a small table. He spoke Spanish and kept calling for salt. No one was paying any attention to him. Something about his appearance reminded Lupe of her uncle Gus. She noticed two saltshakers at the ladies' table where she sat and reached for one, then passed it to him.

"*Sal?*" she said. He grunted and began to shake the small bottle over his dinner plate.

"His name is not Sol or Sal or anything like that." One of the silver-haired ladies corrected Lupe. "And he's not supposed to eat salt. Hypertension, you know." Lupe didn't appreciate being corrected. The man was old. What harm was it to give him what he was asking for? "Can you get me some more iced tea, dearie?" Did this lady who directed the whole table think that Lupe was there to wait on her? She needed to get away.

"Excuse me. I'm going to wash my hands." Lupe used the excuse to leave the table. As she got up to leave, she could see that Penny was already plowing into her plate of chicken. She let the old ladies fawn over her. Lupe went in search of the ladies' room, hoping to hide her temper and discomfort.

By the time dessert was being served, Lupe was on her way back to the table. The sales lady, Ginny Rogers, spotted Lupe and approached her. Apparently, she was observing how the girls mixed in with the residents.

"I saw you talking with Mr. Ramirez. He never talks to anyone. He speaks mostly Spanish, you know."

"I just gave that man salt. He was asking for it. Sorry if that was wrong." How could she ever endure sixty hours of this place? She felt like Ginny was specifically watching her. Lupe looked like the servers or the cleaners, but not like any of the residents except this man in the wheelchair, whom everyone ignored.

"Don't worry about it. Does your family speak Spanish? Where were you born?" Ginny's questions poured out of her. "It would be so good for Mr. Ramirez to have a friend to talk to." Did this sales lady ever ask the servers to talk to him? Did she realize that Mama, and probably a lot of the other workers, could be a friend to this man?

"I'll try." Lupe said what she thought Ginny wanted to hear, but she had no intention of befriending this old man or anyone else in this place.

The next week at school, Ms. Granger called out to Lupe and Penny as they made their way to their third-period class.

"They loved you!" She flashed an animated thumbs-up. "This is perfect. I'm so glad you are doing the service hours." The girls feigned smiles and waved back to the counselor.

"That woman needs to get a life," Lupe muttered.

"Come on, it's not so bad." Penny grinned and greeted everyone she passed in the hall like Ms. Personality. The girls headed toward the gym, and Lupe glared straight ahead. "You're the one who said we'd be at the university sports camp soon. Chill, girl. So how's your old fat man?"

"Mr. Ramirez. I told you his name."

"You know I can't remember all those names—Alvarez, Perez, all those Z names."

Lupe knew exactly what she meant but chose not to pursue it. Penny had completed two years of Spanish but couldn't speak a word of it. Lupe thought it was a choice Penny made and not for the best reasons. On the other hand, Lupe remembered the silver-haired ladies' names—Gladys, Nancy, and Susie—even though they had overlooked her and loved Penny, who would worm her way into an inheritance from them before the girls finished their community service hours.

"Well, Mr. Ramirez is okay if you don't mind seeing his dinner stuck on the front of his shirt. Or if you don't mind the curly black hairs that snake out of his ears and nose. Or mind that he falls asleep in the middle of a conversation, and when he wakes up, he asks the same question."

"The ladies are fun; we play cards." Penny snacked on some cookies she smuggled out of the Villa. "Really? What does he ask?"

"He asked why the school allows girls to play softball. Can you believe that?" Lupe recalled the conversation. She poked her finger in the air, imitating Raul making his point.

"For him baseball is the only sport. He thinks he's the specialist and only men can play!"

"Did you tell him about Title IX?" Penny stood still and looked at Lupe in disbelief. "How old do you think he is? Doesn't he know girls get equal rights in sports?" Penny was indignant.

"Well, honestly, my Spanish isn't that good. It kind of limits what I can say to him." Lupe held out her hand for half of Penny's cookie.

Santa Barbara Sporting News

A Roll Call from Our Local Teams

Spring 1994

Students in the Community

High School seniors from every part of the state are fulfilling their mandated community service requirement (CSR) hours, as established by assembly member Judith Cranz (AB789) in 1980.

The student volunteers gain valuable work experience and provide much needed staffing power to hundreds of local projects, small business, and healthcare facilities. From recreational facilities to hospital reception lobbies, local students can be seen lending a hand and gaining valuable skills in addition to their final year of academic studies in our local high schools, both public and private.

If your program or office can provide CSR hours to local students, you can make arrangements by calling SBHS Counselor, Leslie Granger at (555) 689-7034.

CHAPTER 4

The next evening when the girls arrived at the Villa, Mr. Ramirez was not in the dining room. Ginny asked Lupe to follow her to the elevator.

"He requested dinner in his room. Why don't you go up and visit? He'd like that." Inside the elevator the air was stuffy. There were papers taped to every wall with calendars, announcements, rules. It felt claustrophobic. The elevator bumped to an abrupt stop on the third floor. Ginny led the way down a hall with more hanging art. Some of the doorways were decorated with wreaths of silk flowers. Some doors just held notepaper and a pen hanging on a string.

"This is Mr. Ramirez's room." They reached a bare door with a greenish light glowing from under the doorway. "I'll just leave you here. Give a little knock before you go in." Was it just Lupe's imagination, or was Ginny afraid to enter Mr. Ramirez's room? Lupe called out and opened the door. A familiar gruff voice responded.

"*Bueno, Lupita? Venga.* Come in."

The place smelled like pine incense. The green glow under the door came from a lighted mirror on the wall. Below the mirror a small china bowl and a little shot glass were placed on a shelf. The bowl appeared to hold a few pieces of Ramirez's dinner, and the glass was half-full of an amber liquid. *Was he allowed to have whiskey in his room?* Lupe wondered.

Mr. Ramirez's wheelchair was positioned in front of a framed picture of a baseball player hung beside the mirror. In the picture, the man was bent on one knee, a bat propped on his shoulder. She stared at the player's face.

"It is his week. I remember him every day, but this is his special week." Mr. Ramirez' words were full of reverence. Lupe had no idea who this old player was. It wasn't a West Coast team uniform; she recognized all of those colors and emblems.

"Who is it?" Lupe asked. Mr. Ramirez stared at her and shook his head and clicked his tongue.

"*Ay, chica.* You tell me you love softball, and yet, you don't know who this is?"

She moved closer to the photo and recognized the same man who held the door for her on her first visit to the Villa, the handsome young man who also called her *chica*.

"Is he your son? I saw him here on my first night."

"This is the most famous player I recruited, in Puerto Rico in 1953. Roberto Clemente. You cannot play ball and not know him." His voice was firm and agitated. "You cannot be a Latino and not know him. And he would never appear to a *tonta*, a fool like you." He was obviously getting angry. She backed away toward the door. "He is a *santo*. A real saint."

"You don't need to yell at me. I'm volunteering to be here, you know." She glared at him and twisted a button on her jacket, trying to hold her temper. Part of her felt foolish. How was she expected to know about a player from so long ago, and why did he call Clemente a saint? All she knew for sure was that she had seen this same man the night she and Penny first entered the front door at the Villa.

Lupe didn't wait for an answer from Mr. Ramirez; instead, she left and headed to the game room, where Penny was playing cards with her silver-haired ladies.

"I'm out of here. Come on." She didn't stop to say a polite good night but instead pushed through the lobby and dug down deep into backpack the minute she reached the sidewalk. She kept a stack of old baseball player cards her brother once gave her for luck. "Roberto Clemente," she muttered the name as she removed the rubber band and shuffled the stack of cards in her hands.

"What's up with you?" Penny struggled to get into her jacket. "We still have over an hour to be here."

"Have you ever heard of a player named Roberto Clemente? Ramirez was going off on me just because I didn't know who he was." Lupe stared at the card she had pulled from the deck.

"Well, yeah. Pittsburgh, I think, a long time ago." Penny zipped up her jacket.

"Look at this." Lupe held up the card in front of Penny's face.

"Hot! Say, he looks like the guy we saw our first night here. Where did you get that old card?" Penny reached for the card, but Lupe pulled it back and read aloud the note below the photo.

"Roberto Clemente, 1934-1972."

"God, he played a long time." Penny squinted at the card. "Wait a minute, that can't be the same guy."

"No kidding, dummy—1972 was the year he died." Lupe felt a chill run down her back and shook her shoulders.

"How weird is that? Do you think this place is haunted?" Penny rubbed the back of her neck.

Later that night, Lupe cleared the dishes and cleaned the kitchen at home. Her mama was ironing in the next room. Their small wood-frame house consisted of the kitchen and dining room, two bedrooms, and an enclosed porch. David and Lupe had shared a room when they were kids; now, he slept on the porch, giving Lupe some privacy in the second bedroom.

"Mama, have you ever seen anything weird happen at the Villa?" Lupe shook the dish towel.

"Like what, *mija*?" Mama ironed at home between her day job and her night job at the Villa.

"That man, Mr. Ramirez, creeps me out. Do you know he has a little altar in his room?" Lupe watched to see if her mother's expression revealed anything.

"A lot of the old people keep family pictures in their room. They're lonely, sweetie. Just think of how it would be if we could not live together in our *casita*. By the way, how are those new shoes working for you? Thank you for keeping them so clean, *mija*." Mama looked up and shared a small smile with Lupe.

"Do other people put little bits of food for their family in front of the photos? He's probably attracting rats." Confused, Lupe glanced at her shoes hanging from her bag. She was sure they had been a mess after practice.

"Oh, that kind of altar. Your grandma used to do that after your grandpa died. She was sure he visited the house every night to keep her safe." Mama picked up Papa's old shot glass. "You remember how we toast your papa sometimes with our orange juice? It's the same thing."

"*Deveras*, really? In Mr. Ramirez's room I saw an altar for some old ball player named Clemente. Don't you think that's weird?" Lupe remembered their orange juice pretend toasts.

"Roberto Clemente?" David entered the kitchen and barged right into the conversation. Since Papa died, they could not predict when David might show up. He'd dropped out of school and cruised around in Papa's old Chevy. When he did come home, he had a lot of small bills, half of which he gave to Mama. "Who do you think my best glove is named after? Roberto! The best fielder ever, played for the Pirates, killed in an airplane crash in Puerto Rico."

"No, Nicaragua," Mama corrected her son. "You weren't even born then. Your papa idolized him. He thought he was a saint."

"That's the thing, so does Mr. Ramirez. He told me unless I knew about this guy, I shouldn't play ball or even call myself a Latina." Lupe stood with her hands on her hips.

"Chicana, little sister." David was always correcting her. Lupe couldn't believe her brother and her own mother, who knew next to nothing about softball, both knew about Clemente.

"It's not so weird, Lupe. Some people never get the kind of love they really need." Mama always ironed her own uniform after finishing her paid ironing work. "Your papa spoiled us all with his love before he passed. Everyone needs someone to look up to, especially an old man who is all alone. You're still going back to the Villa, *deveras*, right?"

Lupe didn't have a choice; she had to finish her hours at the Villa in order to graduate and play ball for the university. Maybe she could hang out with Penny and play cards with the silver-haired ladies. It didn't seem like Mr. Ramirez wanted to be around her any more than she wanted to be around him. Was it just her imagination that made her think they had seen this man, Roberto Clemente, on their first night at the Villa? It was creepy. David naming his glove in honor of Clemente was weird, too. That man said something about her shoes. Had he touched them?

Santa Barbara Sporting News

A Roll Call from Our Local Teams

Spring 1994

Roberto Clemente Day Celebrated by MLB 1994

On Friday, MLB celebrates the 22nd annual Roberto Clemente Day, honoring the legacy of one of baseball's greatest players and humanitarians nearly twenty-two years after his tragic passing. Clemente, a native of Puerto Rico, died in a plane crash at the age of thirty-eight, on New Year's Eve, 1972, while delivering emergency aid to earthquake victims in Nicaragua.

Roberto Enrique Clemente Walker was a Puerto Rican professional baseball player who played eighteen seasons in Major League Baseball for the Pittsburgh Pirates, primarily as a right fielder. After his early and sudden death, the National Baseball Hall of Fame changed its rules so that a player who has been dead for at least six months could be eligible for entry. In 1973, Clemente was posthumously inducted, becoming the first Caribbean and the first Latin-American player to be honored in the Hall of Fame.

CHAPTER 5

The second week of her volunteer service at the Villa, Lupe noticed a pile of newspaper clippings about her softball team at the front desk. Maybe she could get someone to bring Mr. Ramirez to one of her games. She'd show him what a girl could do, that crazy old man.

"Whose clippings are these?" Lupe asked Ginny, who managed the desk that evening. "That's my team, you know."

"Yes, I've seen your photos. I thought they might be from your scrapbook. Someone leaves these for Mr. Ramirez. This week, he started a whole collection on his wall. I find them here each day and put them in his mailbox."

"Actually, I haven't seen Mr. Ramirez for days. Instead of visiting him last week, I played cards with the ladies in the game room after dinner." Lupe fidgeted with the sign-in pen and avoided looking at Ginny. She worried that her volunteer credit might not count unless she spent time with Mr. Ramirez, like Ginny originally requested.

"Well, I hope you see him again soon. In a place like this we never know." Ginny's voice trailed off.

"It would be easier if someone could bring him to one of my games sometime. We're doing really well, and he needs to see how girls can play ball, too." Lupe sorted the clippings.

"You sound a little bossy, Lupe." Ginny looked up, giving Lupe an attitude check.

"Oh, forget it," Lupe said. Her eyes were drawn to someone sitting on the sofa in the lobby—a man clipping stories from the newspaper.

"It would take a special bus for his wheelchair. Is the stadium accessible?" Ginny asked. The man with the newspaper lowered the section he held and looked at Lupe. It was him again, the Clemente man. She froze. He nodded his head as if to say, "Yes, let him see you play."

"What do you mean accessible? Maybe his son could bring him?" Lupe nodded toward the sofa, hoping this man was truly Ramirez's son and not some sort of ghost. Ginny looked toward the sofa, then back at Lupe.

"What do you mean? He doesn't have a son, or anyone, honey. That old high school stadium would not be easy for anyone in a wheelchair." The phone rang and Ginny began another conversation.

Mr. Ramirez never showed up at a game, and it was a good thing because the team's luck turned around and the next two games were disasters. In the third game Crusty Crystal Benson was brought in to replace Lupe as pitcher before the fifth inning. It was humiliating. Crystal practically lived in the weight room when she was not on the field, but since no one had ever seen her enter the gym showers, she got the nickname "Crusty." She had a good arm, but the stronger she got, the more she threw like a pitching robot. The trouble was that she was so consistent, the batters began to get hits off her predictable pitches. The team was going down in flames.

"Did you see the university recruiter back in the stands today? I thought she was all done after we signed our agreements."

Even Penny was nervous about how the season would end and what that meant for the future. Lupe began to panic.

"Do you think they are going to drop us from the team before we even get started? Have you heard something?" This tension didn't help Lupe's pitching performance. She was losing her confidence and her dreams. "I knew it was all too good to be true."

"Tough break, girls." The university recruiter approached the girls after their third loss.

"We can do better. We're just in a slump." Lupe and Penny shifted their weight from foot to foot, slamming the ball into their mitts.

"The end of the season is a bad time for a slump, girls. How is everything else going? Your grades, your community service hours? We're going to have to cut back on scholarship agreements for the players who don't fulfill all the requirements." The recruiter fidgeted with her clipboard and looked uncomfortable.

"Cut back? What does that mean? You promised us!" Lupe heard the panic in her own voice.

"Well, we'll still include you in our training camp. Believe me, it will be a real improvement over this field." Lupe felt a stab of shame about her school's diamond and bleachers. "Your admission is guaranteed, but we may not be able to manage the full scholarship. It's my job to build a winning team." It was obvious the recruiter was not impressed. Even worse, she turned her attention to Crusty Crystal at the first opportunity she had and left the girls hanging. "Hey, Crystal, nice arm."

"This is bad," Penny said.

"It's worse than bad. It's the end. No matter how little she cuts back the scholarship, my mama will not be able to fill the gap. I'm done." Lupe blamed her volunteer time at the Villa for using up her energy and extra practice time.

Santa Barbara Sporting News

A Roll Call from Our Local Teams

Spring 1994

SBHS Softball Hits a Hard Spot: Pitcher Replaced

In an effort to keep the Lady Dons from falling behind in the ranks of girls softball this season, Coach Collins at SBHS is making an important change in the roster. "Each player is stretched thin covering their position, supporting the team as a whole, and trimming back errors," the coach said recently.

"I've got my work cut out for me," she added with a laugh, "but my expectations are just to go a game at a time. The goal is really to start establishing better numbers. So far, we've been doing a pretty good job with that."

Softball at the oldest school in the district has been hamstrung by the lack of any feeder programs. Other local teams have received steady streams of talent from the long-established GSBA league and the summer travel teams it's spawned. The coach's recent decision is to remove pitcher Lupe Lopez from the starting roster and replace her with fastballer Crystal Benson on the mound.

CHAPTER 6

L upe hated playing Rummikub, but residents at the Villa
loved it. In order to avoid visiting with Mr. Ramirez, Lupe
sat next to Penny as she played the game with the silver-haired
ladies. The older women were so used to the game they were
able to keep a conversation going without even pausing to
count up their tiles.

"You know, you young girls are not the first females to
play softball. When I was young, we had a woman softball
player named Dot. What was her last name?" The woman
turned to her friends with better memories. "You remember—
she played lots of sports."

"You're thinking of Billie Jean King." The woman across
the table lay down three tiles at a time and spoke with great
self-confidence.

"We know who she is, but she played tennis, not softball."
Penny winked at Lupe.

"No, this woman played softball—Dot something. It was
before the war," the older woman said.

"Which war?" Penny kept the conversation going, all the
while sneaking Lupe sly smiles.

"Well, World War II, of course. How old do you think we are, dear? Wait a minute . . . Wilkinson, that was her name!" The Villa resident smiled as she regained her memory.

A woman working on a puzzle in the same room had overheard the entire conversation. She raised her voice and called out to the Rummikub players.

"Oh, for goodness' sake, we have a book about Dot Wilkinson in our library. It's right over there." The puzzle player pointed to the far end of the game room, where a jumbled library overflowed with magazines and paperback novels. Lupe stood up and moved toward the shelves that she had previously overlooked.

"Oh, Lynn. How can you find anything on those shelves? Are you sure? Dot Wilkinson?" The Rummikub players never took their eyes off their tiles.

"Of course, I'm sure. I wrote that book." The woman they knew as Alice, with short, cropped salt-and-pepper hair, stood next to the players with her arms crossed over her chest. She turned and followed Lupe to the bookshelves. "It's right there, honey. It's called *Girls Play Ball, Too.*"

"Really? You wrote this?" Lupe had never met a real author and found it hard to believe that this little old lady knew anything about softball. "How did you do that?"

"Dot and I were friends in Arizona when we were young. She told me all her stories. She never had enough money to buy shoes or equipment. She had to work after school to help out her folks. And worst of all was the teasing and rubbish she got from the boys, and even some of the girls, for playing ball."

"Wow, that sounds a lot like me." Lupe turned the book over in her hands. "Can I borrow this book for a school report?"

"You bet, sweetheart. None of the women here want to read about women in sports. You can have it. And if you need any help, just ask me." Alice looked pleased to see Lupe's interest.

"You never know the stories our residents have to tell, right, Alice?" Ginny Rogers entered the game room. "Everyone here has an interesting history, like Mr. Ramirez, for example. How's it going with him, Lupe?"

Had she been watching Lupe to see if she was doing her volunteer job of visiting Mr. Ramirez?

BOOK REPORT

TITLE: *Girls Play Ball, Too*
AUTHOR: Alice Allen
CLASS: History
TEACHER: Mr. Robinson
STUDENT: Lupe Lopez
DATE: May 1, 1994

I read *Girls Play Ball, Too* because it was about a woman who played softball, like me. Her name was Dot Wilkinson, and she played ball a long time ago in the 1930s. She was a good player for the Phoenix Ramblers. She even got into the Hall of Fame.

But Dot still had problems, just like me. First, when she grew up, she was very poor. Her family could not support her athletic goals. She still kept playing many sports. She was determined. Since it was so long ago, she didn't have Title IX that we have today for girls and women in sports. She also had many people—both men and women—who made fun of her for playing. Even so, she was a great catcher. Another famous woman athlete, sports icon, and champion for equality, Billie Jean King, said this about her:

> Dot Wilkinson is the greatest female catcher ever to play softball. A bold, pioneering athlete, she refused to let others define her and instead defined herself. Her story is an inspiration to people everywhere.

Even better, I got to meet the woman who wrote the book about Dot Wilkinson. They were friends when they were kids. Her name is Alice Allen, and she has written other women's sports books and even made a movie. She won awards for her books. She is an old woman now. I met her in my community service assignment at Villa Santa Barbara.

I really like to play softball. I'm a pitcher. I enjoyed reading this book. I never met anyone who wrote a book before. Maybe I'll try to write when I am old and can't pitch anymore.

CHAPTER 7

The softball team members were expected to take turns working the women's sports table at the weekly flea market to raise money for the team activities. Each Saturday morning, the student parking lot at the high school was transformed with vendors selling goods, new and used—everything from tacos to toasters.

"Less chatting and more selling, girls." Coach Collins supervised. "Five minutes to eleven; half price starts then. Be ready."

"I like her better on the field than I do bossing us around here." Penny rearranged the china mugs, picture frames, and all the cast-off goods collected from the garages, attics, and basements of the players' parents. Lupe was amazed at how much junk these other families had accumulated. Mama never donated, but she bought stuff when it was time for the half-price sale.

"Look at them, just lurking around for the cheap stuff." Crusty Crystal eyed the shoppers as she worked alongside Penny and Lupe. "Who would buy any of this junk? It's really kind of disgusting."

Most of the other players shared Crystal's view of the swap meet. It was hard to get them to work the table, but everyone knew the dollars they made went right into the team travel budget. They grudgingly agreed to get their parents to donate items for sale but hated to work the table. Lupe stood toward the back of the booth, hoping her mother would not show up. This was where she did most of her weekend shopping, and Lupe didn't want anyone to know it.

"Half price!" When Penny cupped her hands around her mouth and called out, the table was overrun with eager buyers, and Lupe had to step forward to help the others.

"This is stupid. If we don't win this week, we're not going to be traveling to any more games." Lupe leaned toward Penny as she complained.

"I heard that, Lupe." Coach Collins stood behind the girls. "What we make here is not just for this season. You know what I always say."

"'Take one for the team.' We know." Lupe and Penny muttered her motto. Their hands were busy collecting dollars and coins until finally the customers slowed down and the job of packing up the leftover goods began.

"Lupe! Lupe Lopez, *dónde estás?*" Mama's voice rang out, and Lupe's embarrassment turned her face red.

"*Aquí, Mama.*" She left the booth and tried to meet her mother someplace out of view of the others. "What's the matter? You know I'm busy."

"It's your brother," Mama blurted out and Lupe held her breath. "He's been in an accident." Mama grabbed Lupe's arm and pulled her toward the street. "We're going to the hospital now."

Lupe's face changed from hot red to cold white in an instant. There was no time to get more details or say goodbye to Penny. She followed Mama toward the Chevy parked nearby. *At least it wasn't a car crash,* she thought. *But what?*

"What happened to him?" Lupe stood back from David's hospital bed while Mama smoothed his hair and straightened his sheets. He slept, his face bruised and swollen. His right arm, his pitching arm, was in a cast that went all the way down to his hand. "Did he fall?"

"Hush, *mija*. The doctor said they could operate, but we don't have the money. He said the bones may mend in this cast so he can use his arm again." Mama avoided answering Lupe's question.

Lupe was not sure she really wanted to know what had happened. What she did know was that the problem was about money again. *Everything comes down to money*, she thought.

She couldn't keep her eyes off the cast on David's arm. She knew he loved playing baseball. Lupe remembered when David used to let her chase foul balls when he and his friends played in a nearby field. Some of her best memories were from the year he taught her to throw, then catch, and finally, swing the bat. After Papa died of a heart attack, David gave Lupe her first pitching lessons. He used to tease her, saying, "Lupe throws like a girl." But later, he encouraged her to try out for the team.

Mama drove the Chevy to the hospital for the next two days, and they spent all day with David. The car was one way that Lupe and her mama could still feel close to Papa. He rebuilt the classic 1957 sedan with parts he collected from the junkyard when Lupe and her brother were in grammar school. He never seemed to worry about money, like Mama. "We can just use what we have, our family and the brains God gave us," Papa used to say. Sure enough, Mama hand-stitched the seat covers with remnants from a local upholstery shop. The car's patchwork paint job, not classic but inexpensive, made the car unmistakable with three tones of green set off by black accent stripes.

CHAPTER 8

After the weekend, David was released from the hospital in his cast with strict rules about his pain medications. On the first day he was home, Lupe noticed police cruisers on the street but thought little about it. Their neighborhood was no stranger to regular patrols. Lupe moved her own things out on the porch so her brother could have her bedroom. Mama left the Chevy parked at the curb so David could look out the window and see it.

"It feels odd to be home during the week." Mama refreshed David's pillow and water pitcher. "Is there always this much traffic?"

"Sometimes on school holidays." Lupe could see something was bothering her mother.

"Lupe, remember when you asked me about weird things happening?" Mama spoke slowly, and she glanced at David to see if he was sleeping. "When we checked out of the hospital, the clerk said the bill was already paid. I was even thinking of selling your papa's Chevy to pay for it. It had to be a lot of money after several days."

"You wouldn't ever sell Papa's car, would you?" Lupe thought there was some sort of health insurance, but Mama told her there was no such thing.

"I think the people at the hospital made a mistake. We'll just enjoy the old car for as long as we can."

The next day, Lupe returned to school and softball practice. Afterward, she dragged herself back to the Villa, determined to complete her hours and be eligible to graduate. Mr. Ramirez was waiting for her in the lobby when she arrived.

"How's David? When Roberto told me about him, we lit a candle." He looked so sincere Lupe could not work up the energy to tell him she thought he was crazy and didn't want to hear any more about his ghost.

"Thanks, but how did you really find out?" Lupe glanced around the lobby and saw that they were alone. "You might as well know, I don't believe anything about this Santo Roberto business. I think it's ridiculous to have a shrine in your room, but right now I could really use some help, no matter where it comes from."

"If you understood you would not think it's silly," Mr. Ramirez said. "He helps me."

"Okay, if you've got to talk about him, tell me about Roberto Clemente. Maybe I can get a paper out of this for school. I'm trying to improve my grade point average to get that scholarship." *How many more visits to the Villa can I stand?* she thought.

That evening, Lupe's education about the history of baseball and Latino players began. Mr. Ramirez showed her his press clippings, old letters, and photos. It turned out to be true. He actually did recruit Roberto Clemente and other players into the National League.

"It was the best—and worst—job I ever had. The League managers pressured me to find the best talent and the whitest-looking players, then we offered the players the lowest-paying contracts. The kids like Roberto desperately wanted to come to the US and play in the big leagues. When they got here, they learned that it was not easy for them to be away from their families or face the prejudices in this country."

Besides Roberto Clemente, who played for Pittsburgh, Mr. Ramirez told Lupe about Manny Mota, who mainly played for the San Francisco Giants, and Fernando Valenzuela, who was a famous Dodgers player. She shuffled through all his old papers and found a player named Juan Marichal from the Dominican Republic. She also saw news clippings for players named Carew and Rivera from Panama, and more.

"But this was so long ago, in the 1960s and '70s." Lupe dug into boxes of baseball memorabilia. "What's this story about an all-star team of Dominicans playing in the major leagues?" Lupe sorted the clippings and began to think about her assignments in her history class. Mr. Robinson, her history teacher, kept telling her to find something she was interested in and write about it. She told him she was only interested in softball, but maybe this stuff would come in handy.

"I have hundreds of stories I could tell you if you really want to know. I even ran a baseball camp in the Dominican Republic to get the kids ready to get started in the minor leagues. Look here." Mr. Ramirez held up a photo of a young player hitting an old tire hanging from a tree. "That was our homemade batting practice. We used what we had and the brains God gave us." For a moment Lupe thought she was listening to her own papa. Then Ramirez took a golden plaque out of a tattered old suitcase.

"After a lot of work for the league, this was presented to me at the Baseball Hall of Fame in Cooperstown, New York."

"Aren't you rich after all this? How did you end up here?" She looked around at his small room. He had a few shirts in the closet, but above those shirts was a row of baseball caps, each from a different team and each with at least one player's signature.

"Rich with memories and some old friends, like Roberto," Mr. Ramirez said.

"But your room is like a little museum. Haven't you ever thought of selling this stuff? These hats and shirts are probably worth some money." Mr. Ramirez's altar to Roberto Clemente took up most of the space on one wall, and now he had pinned Lupe's press clippings and photo right next to Roberto's. "Looks like you decided girls can play ball." She gazed at her team photo with pride. "Tell me the truth: Did you really light a candle for David? He loved to play ball. He taught me."

"Yes, we did. I only wish I had met David earlier. He could have been a major league player." Mr. Ramirez hung his head.

From that day on Lupe returned to see Mr. Ramirez daily and took notes for her history papers from his clippings. When she explained her project to her teacher, Mr. Robinson, he could not have been more excited. At the end of the school year she would earn her first A in history.

Something else changed. Lupe began to notice that Roberto Clemente was watching her team practices, but she didn't want to mention this to Mr. Ramirez. If he really was dead like the newspaper said, why was he here and how long would he hang around? She could see that Mr. Ramirez looked weaker each time she visited.

"Our last game is Friday. Do you think you can make it?" Lupe asked Mr. Ramirez on her next visit.

"We've been thinking about it," he said. Lupe didn't want to ask him who he meant when he said "we" because she knew.

"Do you think he can help you get to the game?" Lupe avoided saying Clemente's name.

"Normally he coaches the outfielders down at the East Side Field on Friday afternoon, but he said he would try if you wanted us there."

"Now you're kidding me," she said.

"You and your brother are not the only people we worry about. Life is not always fair, Lupe." Mr. Ramirez was gazing up at his Roberto Clemente shrine as he spoke. "Just when you think you've moved up to the next level, something drags you down." Something in his voice told her that more trouble was coming.

BOOK REPORT

TITLE: *Clemente!*
AUTHOR: Kal Wagenheim
CLASS: History
TEACHER: Mr. Robinson
STUDENT: Lupe Lopez
DATE June 5, 1994

Roberto Clemente was born in 1934 in Puerto Rico. His father was very poor. His mother did other people's laundry to earn money. His father was a sugarcane cutter and had six other children. Roberto was the youngest child in the family. He helped his father load his truck and also worked for the neighbors so he could buy rubber balls. He loved to play all sports. I liked that this book gave me some information about Roberto's childhood.

Baseball was very popular in Puerto Rico. The sugarcane plantations had their own teams that played one another. Baseball was Roberto's favorite game. He was able to watch the American teams when they came to Puerto Rico to play in the summer league. Roberto was Black, and he especially liked to see players from the Negro leagues. The book did not say this, but it seems like Black players and white players were treated differently in those days.

In 1952 Roberto Clemente got his first contract to play for a Puerto Rican team. He was only eighteen years old. In those days the Dodgers played for Brooklyn in New York. They signed Clemente in

1954, but he did not end up staying there too long. In 1954 the Pittsburgh Pirates drafted Clemente. That same year, he was in a car accident and his brother died of a brain tumor. It's sad, but it helps to know that even famous ball players also have their share of problems.

In 1960 Clemente hit sixteen home runs for the Pirates and made the National League All-Star team. Then Clemente had a hit in all seven of the World Series games against the New York Yankees, and the team won the series.

That is all very important to sports history, but the best part about Roberto Clemente was that he always stood up for the little guy and went out of his way to help others. He was an inspiration to Puerto Rican kids and everybody else. It was so sad to read about his big heart, which is what eventually took him out of the game.

When Roberto was coaching the winter league in Puerto Rico in 1972, a huge earthquake hit Nicaragua. Wanting to help the victims of that earthquake, Roberto collected donations of food and medicine and hired a plane to deliver the donations. He was on the plane when it crashed on New Year's Eve and he lost his life.

In 1973 Roberto was the first player from Latin America to be inducted into the Baseball Hall of Fame. This book had a lot of baseball statistics, but I think the parts about what a good man Roberto was were the most important.

CHAPTER 9

Lupe thought about how Roberto Clemente had died on her way home from the Villa. No wonder people called him a saint. She tried to recall what David and Mama had said about him. As she approached the house, the street seemed dark and still. It was kind of spooky, given the details of Clemente's death were on her mind. When she stepped onto the porch, expecting to find David and Mama inside, car doors slammed, dogs barked, headlights flashed on, a van pulled up, and a light shone from inside the house.

"Stay right where you are. Put your hands in the air!" Two police officers approached the porch, one man with his hand on his gun holster and a woman with a flashlight in one hand and her badge in the other. The man also held a German Shepherd that strained against its leash. They made a racket, and when Mama opened the door, fear was etched into her features.

"Identify yourself. What is your business here?" The policewoman spoke to Lupe, then turned her attention toward Mama, who held her hand in front of her mouth. David peeked around her.

"That's my daughter. What do you want?" Mama's voice shook. She held her arm out to protect David; with the other arm she reached toward Lupe.

"Is that your Chevy at the curb? Are you David Lopez, sir?" This time it was the officer holding the dog who spoke to David. Two other officers were crossing the street toward the house. Neighbors peered out from their porches.

"That is my husband's car," Mama said. David, supporting his arm in the cast, stepped out onto the porch. "Put that animal away. You don't need it here," Mama spoke boldly.

"Is your husband in the house, ma'am? Is his name David Lopez?" Now there were four officers, two on the walkway, one with a dog on the steps, and the woman on the porch. Lupe had not moved an inch.

"My husband is dead." Lupe could not recall her mother ever saying this out loud, even though Papa had been gone for a year. "Tell us what you want. You are frightening my children."

"We have two warrants to serve here: one for the arrest of a David Lopez, and the other to impound this 1957 Chevy, California license plate number APF2349." The officer took a step toward David.

"I can explain this Mama, believe me." David looked afraid.

Mama convinced the police to come inside after they handcuffed David in front of the whole neighborhood. Lupe thought of running to find some help. But who was there to help?

The faint clicking sound was all the noise those handcuffs made restraining David's good arm with a metal ring linked to a chain around his waist. Hands that threw a baseball, hands that lifted her younger self into a chair.

Mama's rigid smile stayed in place. Her careful courtesy was interspersed with the clipped, rigid statements of the police. Their eyes scanned every corner of the small living room, searched toward the hallway, and pierced into the kitchen, where David's baseball glove, Roberto, lay on the table next to *Abuela* Alicia's photo.

Mama spoke as if the intruders were company out for a neighborhood walk with their mad dog. How could she remain calm with her son in handcuffs? How could she do anything else?

Lupe stood with her back in the corner, near the old wall heater that clicked on each December. Why did she feel guilty? The frail edge of her life without Papa, her world that pretended to be normal, crumbled under her feet as her brother was led out.

She glanced across the street, and she saw him, Roberto Clemente, standing on a neighbor's lawn, as clear as day. Did he have something to do with this? Would he be able to help?

Santa Barbara Sporting News

A Roll Call from Our Local Teams

Spring 1994

Local Man Connected to Robbery Arrest

Local police confirm a man has been arrested in connection with three separate robberies in recent weeks. *Sporting News* reports this incident, having corroborated several news clippings regarding the athletic excellence of the arrestee in the prior twelve months.

The thefts took place in different neighborhoods. Each time, a suspicious car was identified and reported to police. The registered owner of that vehicle is the late David Macias Lopez. The man's son, David Lopez Jr., was arrested without resistance in his home last Wednesday.

According to the police record, Lopez Jr. was recently released from Midtown Hospital, where he had been treated for multiple contusions, a mild concussion, and a broken arm. A 1957 Chevrolet, corresponding to the description given by police tipsters, was impounded at the time of the arrest.

CHAPTER 10

"Do I have to stay at home alone tonight?" Lupe put on a brave face until the police left with David. Everything the police had told Mama explained David's broken arm, bruised face, and now his arrest. It was not a good story, but now she knew what had happened.

After Papa died, David thought he was responsible for the family. As a high school dropout, his ability to get a job was limited. He'd agreed to help out some of his old friends from school. Unfortunately what they wanted him to do was to be a lookout for them. All he had to do was cruise the neighborhoods that they planned to rob and call them if he spotted police in the area.

For a few weeks he brought home extra money for Mama to cover the rent. After the rent was paid, he didn't show up for his job as a lookout. His old friends told him he could not quit. They tracked him down in the Chevy one evening, blaming him when a home alarm went off and two of his friends were arrested. The others got away, dragged him out of the car, and beat him up.

That was how he ended up in the hospital. As long as David was in the hospital, he was able to hide from the gang. But they weren't done with him yet. When he came home to recuperate, the Chevy was parked on the street, and it was a dead giveaway for the thugs and for the police. The police got to the house first, and now David was under arrest.

Lupe was relaying the horror of the arrest on the phone to Penny while her mama got ready for work, just as if it was a normal night. Penny seemed especially quiet when Lupe retold the scary events during the arrest of her brother.

"Was it on Saturday? Are you sure?" she asked. "Did they say how they knew it was him?"

"It wasn't him stealing stuff, Penny! It was just some dumbass who reported his car in their precious neighborhood." Lupe blurted out her anger, knowing that she couldn't blame Penny for what happened.

In reality, it was Penny's fault. She listened, unable to confess to Lupe that she was the one who had recognized David's car in her neighborhood the night before his arrest. She hadn't thought there was anything wrong about it when she pointed him out to her father. "Look, that's the cool car Lupe's brother drives," she had said. It must have been her dad who'd called the cops.

"But do you really have to work tonight, Mama? What if those men who beat up David come here while you are gone?" Lupe grabbed David's bat and dragged it behind her. She hadn't noticed that he kept it by his bed after he returned home with a broken arm.

"Well, you can come with me, but I've got to show up." Mama's voice shook, and her hands, too. Mama had no bail money, so David had to stay in jail awaiting his arraignment. "Bring your homework. They know you at the Villa. You can work in the game room." Mama moved slowly, but she was determined to keep working. "All we can do right now is work and wait. Let's get going; we'll have to walk."

Lupe was grateful to hear the iron gate clang shut when they entered the Villa's underground garage. Mama headed to the laundry room and pointed Lupe to the door that led to the lobby. The hallways, dining room, and lobby seemed so different at night.

"Hi, Lupe. I didn't expect to see you here tonight. Everyone's gone to bed already." One clerk was at the front desk. Thank goodness she remembered Lupe and the front doors were securely locked.

"I came with my mama. She does the laundry." Lupe was not ashamed to say so tonight. "Can I study here while she works?"

"Your mom works here? I never knew that. Sure, use the game room tables. Would you like some lemonade or a cookie? Just sit behind the desk while I dash to the kitchen." The woman left Lupe feeling like she was in charge. All the fancy pictures, lamps, furniture, and rugs were hers for a moment in this grand, empty, safe lobby.

The only assignment she had for homework was her final essay on her plans after graduation. Lupe stared down at the blank paper, her body curled over the table, her face inches from her pen.

"I plan to bail my brother out of jail," she wrote. It was meant to be funny, but her lips were tight. She crumpled up the paper and shoved it into her bag. "I plan to win the lottery so we never have to worry about money again." This made her smile for a moment. "I plan to be less critical of my mama and her job." She shifted in her chair, lifting herself up. She thought, *I'll do anything to make money as long as I can still play ball—anything except help robbers.*

"I plan to meet my real-life hero, Lisa Fernandez." Lupe began to recall all the special commentary on Fernandez during her televised games. Meeting her role model was a true goal, but one she could not imagine happening in her lifetime. She wrote down all the records, all the honors, all the details of Lisa Fernandez's career in softball that she could recall. Then she lay down her head on the table and dreamed of how they could possibly meet.

"I didn't expect to see you here so late, Lupita. *Que paso*—what are you doing?" Lupe jumped when Mr. Ramirez rolled into the game room in his wheelchair. He wore pajama bottoms and a Dodgers sweatshirt. In his lap he carried a plastic bag. "I need to leave this at the front desk for someone. Is your mama working . . . tonight?" The way he asked about Mama made her think that he already knew what had happened to David. "She has always been very kind to me, even though I rarely get to see her." Lupe hadn't thought he knew Mama at all. He had never mentioned it.

"Did you say that Roberto Clemente spends his afternoons at the East Side Field? You told me that when you said he could not bring you to my last game." Lupe was beginning to think that if the ballplayer was really a saint, maybe he could help the family.

"So now you think you can talk to Roberto?" Mr. Ramirez gloated. "I didn't say he could not bring me to your game; I said he was busy. He's always doing something for others."

"Well, whatever. I have some questions for your saint." She put her head down and pretended to write. "I have homework to do. Good night." She watched Mr. Ramirez roll out toward the front desk and overheard him tell the clerk, "Someone will pick this up in the morning. I wrote her name here."

Mama's shift was over at 6:00 a.m. She found Lupe asleep with her head on the table, drooling on her paper.

"Time to go home, *mija*. The chef gave me some toast. Here." Mama put a fat slice of bread with butter and cinnamon in front of Lupe. She woke up right away. "We can go out the front door today." Lupe grabbed her bag and the toast, then followed her mama. When they were almost out the door, Lupe turned to the night clerk.

"Thanks for the lemonade and cookie last night. Did Mr. Ramirez leave something for me?" She wanted to know what was in that bag he carried.

"No, the note says it's for Penny Williams. She's your friend, right?" The desk clerk said.

"I thought she was." Lupe began to wonder if Penny was keeping secrets from her.

BOOK REPORT

TITLE: *Lisa Fernandez*
SOURCE: Lisa Fernandez- Encyclopedia Britannica
CLASS: History
TEACHER: Mr. Robinson
STUDENT: Lupe Lopez
DATE June 8, 1994

Since Mr. Robinson said we could look up something we wanted to do over the summer, or someone we were interested to meet, I looked up my softball hero, Lisa Fernandez, in the Encyclopedia Britannica. This was harder than I thought it would be.

My first two book reports were from old books, and they were not too hard to read. I did have to decide on the most important parts for the reports. But when I looked up Lisa Fernandez in the Encyclopedia *Britannica*, the article went on and on.

That made this report more difficult to write. At first, I wanted to see all her photographs, because I love looking at how she pitches a softball since I am a pitcher, too. Then I read about her career history, and there was a lot to know. It was too much for me to keep track of, and it is hard to make this report from all that material.

First, I know that she was born in California, like me. I thought that was important. Second, she is Latina like me. That was really important to me, even though her parents are from Cuba and Puerto Rico, and my parents are from Mexico. Also, she had an older brother who played baseball, and that is how she became interested in softball. That is exactly like me, and I thought that was very cool.

Something was very different in Lisa's family. Both her parents played ball. Her mother even coached her brother's team. I could only imagine what it would be like.

So for this report it is important to know that she played all her life. She played in school as a kid and in high school, too. Then she went to college at UCLA and played for them. They won a lot of championships, and she set all kinds of records. I didn't find what she studied in college.

After college graduation she played on the US Women's National Team in the Summer Olympics several times, and the team won gold medals. She also played in the National Pro Fast Pitch League.

No wonder she returned as a coach to UCLA when her professional playing years were done. She even coached the US Women's National Team. After all that, she won the Women's Sports Foundation's Sportswoman of the Year award.

CHAPTER 11

"I can't believe how clueless you are." Lupe was bursting to pick a fight with Penny. She threw her uniform in the locker and jammed in her shoes afterward.

"Hey, don't blame me just because this turned out to be a crummy last day of high school." Penny was already suiting up for the game, two hours early. All Lupe could think about was what Mr. Ramirez left for Penny in that plastic bag at the Villa. What was it? Why hadn't he told her about it?

"Right. We'll probably lose this game, and that geeky recruiter will yank our scholarship." Lupe spit out her words.

"Well, at least we have graduation tomorrow." Penny lowered her chin and looked straight at Lupe. "Come on. My grandparents flew in to see the game and the graduation ceremony. They want pictures of us in our uniforms this afternoon."

"Well, that's just great. Come on, Penny. You might as well tell me what you are hiding from me and why you are going behind my back with Mr. Ramirez!"

"That's supposed to be a surprise." Penny stood up straight and grabbed her backpack. "How did you find out about it?"

"What was in the bag, Penny?" Lupe reached for Penny's backpack, and the two girls tugged back and forth. "Is it in here? Let me see."

"I don't have them anymore." Penny let the pack fall to the ground. "Check it if you don't believe me. I sold them at the hobby shop. My dad buys all kinds of sports stuff there. They went fast."

Lupe squinted at her friend, trying to figure out what she was saying.

"He said you were the one who gave him the idea. Now your brother can come to graduation, right?"

The locker room door swung open. Coach Collins chattered to someone following her.

"Is everyone decent? We have some grandparents with a camera looking for a certain catcher. Penny? Lupe? Is everything okay?"

"We'll talk about this later," Lupe grumbled and headed toward the door. "I'm going to the East Side Field right now. I'll be back in time for the game." She pushed past Penny's grandparents and the coach, saving the rest of her anger for Roberto Clemente when she found him at the field. If he really was a saint, why wasn't he doing anything to help?

Lupe rushed off campus, forgetting she didn't have a way to get to the East Side Field and return in time for the game. The Chevy was impounded. She would wear herself out completely if she tried to run twenty blocks down and twenty blocks back. She spotted a guy from her history class getting in his car and walked toward him, intending to ask him for a ride but chickened out at the last moment. Then she heard a familiar engine approaching.

The most uncool thing a graduating senior could do was ride on the public bus. But what did she care if anyone saw her? This was the last day of school, her brother was in jail, and she was on her way to pick a fight with a ghost. She dug in her bag for her old bus pass, unused since the season began.

The bus route went right to the East Side Field. It was in a neighborhood with houses that were even smaller than hers. After school and weekend games were played here, the Boys & Girls Club games, and sometimes the YMCA kids. The place was packed.

There were no uniforms, but somehow the players and even the coaches and parents all looked the same: short, dark, and not too fit. These kids played in anything they happened to have on. She walked behind a dugout, really just a splintery bench, and could see that all the equipment was mismatched and beaten up.

Lupe couldn't really ask for Roberto Clemente by name, so she walked the perimeter of all four diamonds whose outfields overlapped in the middle of the park. The third right fielder she saw was Clemente. He stood by a kid half his size and showed him how to run, bend, and scoop up oncoming ground balls. His eyes locked on hers as she approached. It occurred to her that she had seen him many times but never talked to him. So she just blurted out, "I've got some questions for you, Roberto Clemente."

"Have you come to help? I thought you had a game today?"

"I'll get there, but first I need some answers from you." This was weird. Was she really talking to the ghost of the famous outfielder at the East Side Field?

"Meet me at the foul line." Clemente patted his young protégé on the back and began his trot toward Lupe.

The teams on the field completed three innings before the things Roberto Clemente was telling Lupe began to make any sense.

"You said you met David here three years ago? How?" Lupe didn't know David ever played here.

"It was right after I came to town with Raul. I owe that man a lot for everything he did for me. I knew he would need a friend when he moved to the Villa. It was not the type of life he was used to, you know—no more locker rooms, ballplayers, training camps. When someone helps you, like he helped me, they become a part of your life forever," Roberto explained.

"But what brought you to this field? And what was my brother doing here? He was still in school. Papa was alive then." Lupe felt a pain in her chest when she thought of her papa.

"He was doing the same thing you are doing at the Villa—community service hours. He coached and he loved it. Your brother even thought of getting certified in sports medicine after graduation. Then you know what happened." Roberto was still watching the outfielder.

"Everything went into the toilet, that's what happened." Lupe watched the kids and wished she was young again.

"I was here because I wanted to stay in the game. The truth is, the big leagues were real tough on me. I got criticized for everything, from the color of my skin and my hot temper to the way I spoke English." Roberto didn't look at Lupe but kept his eye on the outfielder. "When I coach kids, I get to remember the real joy of the game. I need that."

"I never think about major league players having any problems. You all look so confident and self-assured." Lupe noticed a faraway look in Roberto's eyes, as if he was remembering something sad.

"I know you feel like you have a lot of problems, Lupe, but just look at these kids. I believe if I have a chance to do something good for people and don't do it, then I'm wasting my time." Roberto's eyes met hers.

"You could do something good for me. I need to know, were you around when David got beaten up? I saw you the night he was arrested." Lupe faced him.

"I'm the one who called the ambulance. The police finally picked up those jerks yesterday. They won't be around here for a long time." Roberto patted Lupe on the back, just as he had done with the kid playing right field. "You better get back to your game. I have a good feeling about it." His hand on her back felt normal, like a real friend reaching out to touch her.

Santa Barbara Sporting News

A Roll Call from Our Local Teams

Spring 1994

Local Players Head Out to CA Universities

Senioritis has struck the SBHS softball team. Veteran players recently shared plans for their college destinations that include several notable California university teams known for furthering academic and athletic careers. The top three beneficiaries of SBHS athletic talents are Claremont University, Irvine University, and California State University at San Diego.

"Our players have been scouted, ranked, and invited to join some of the most prestigious universities in the state," Coach Collins declared with obvious pride.

Other players will join the emerging softball program at SB City College this fall, and our community will continue to enjoy their performance.

CHAPTER 12

When Lupe got back to campus, she encountered her geometry teacher near the gym. She dreaded having a conversation with Mr. Andrews, but her grade in that class was crucial. The university player contract required a 3.5 grade point average, as well as community service and a high school diploma. This was one of Lupe's worst weeks in high school. She desperately hung on to the promise of her university player's contract.

"What is this paper, Lupe? In my class we do geometry, we don't write about it," Mr. Andrews said. "I know you play ball. I also know the size and shape of the field, but your paper, if you can even call it that"—he waved her thousand-word essay, "The Geometry of Baseball," in the air—"this paper has nothing to do with our class or your poor test scores."

"But I'm trying, Mr. Andrews. Softball makes sense to me, not geometry. I have to pass this class to play at the university. Can't you please count the paper?" Failing the paper for Mr. Andrew's geometry class could ruin her hopes for a 3.5 GPA.

After that depressing conversation, Lupe had to face one more game and one more stupid conversation with the seniors in the dugout. Everyone wanted to talk about graduation, and no one wanted to concentrate on the game.

"So what are you getting for graduation? Where are you going to celebrate?"

"My brother is getting a new GMC truck, and I'm getting his Volkswagen bus." Carrie, who played first base, seemed satisfied with that deal.

The team was already so far behind in the standings Lupe knew they had given up any hope of a win. The seniors were focused on the summer and next year. It was obvious Coach Collins was sizing up the younger players for next season's lineup. She made notes on her clipboard and did nothing to help the older players on the field. In the dugout, Penny chatted with the other seniors.

"Our family is leaving for Europe next week. Dad made it a graduation gift for everyone." The shortstop, Megan, made it sound like this was a reasonable reward for finishing high school.

"My grandparents are so excited to be here they promised to give me a full ride to the U of C. Lupe and I were trying for a scholarship, but I doubt that is going to happen anymore." Penny shared her excitement with the whole team before saying anything to Lupe.

"So long, Lupe," the shortstop snorted. The other girls laughed, even Penny.

When Lupe heard Penny's news, she felt like leaving pitching to Crusty Crystal for the last few innings.

"Coach, how about putting Crystal in? It's the last game." *What do I care,* Lupe thought. *Let the team lose their last game.*

"Good thinking, Lupe. You don't mind?" Coach Collins as oblivious to the dugout conversation.

"Wow, that's really nice of you." Penny tried to compliment Lupe.

"Yeah, sure. And thanks so much for leaving me dangling out on a limb by myself." Lupe moved to the end of the bench and looked away from the team. Penny followed her and sat down.

"I saw Mr. Andrews waiting for you. Is that what's got you so mad? I wish you would have let me help you with that geometry paper." Penny tried to console Lupe.

"I thought Mr. Andrews would at least give me some credit for my paper," Lupe said. "That would have helped my stupid grade. But that's not what I'm mad about."

"At least you won't be the only one not going to the university . . ." Penny began.

"What do you mean?" Lupe could hear some reluctance in Penny's voice. What else had she been hiding?

"My grandparents came to see our game because they wanted to surprise me. They told me they would pay my tuition to the university at Irvine. It's down south near their house. I really always wanted to go there."

Lupe tried to act happy for Penny. She realized, even if she passed geometry, this was the last game they would ever play together.

The only good thing about the game was seeing Mama in the stands. Lupe caught her eye and waved furiously. Mama had taken time away from work to see this last game. To Lupe's surprise, David sat next to her, watching all the action on the field.

"David!" Lupe screamed with a thumbs-up. How did he get released from jail? Her spirits were revived after Penny's betrayal.

The moment the game was over, the rest of the team gathered for a last high five, but Lupe didn't care to stick around for that. She rushed to the stands to see David. Climbing the bleachers, she came face-to-face with the university recruiter.

"Oh, Lupe, do you have a minute? Too bad about the loss. I'm sorry I have to tell you this."

Lupe knew what she was about to say and didn't even let her finish. As long as David was out of jail and Mama was here, Lupe was happy.

"I get it. You're dropping me, right? Well, I've got other things to do anyway." She lied about having any plan after graduation. All she wanted to do now was get to David and Mama.

"You do? I know some other coaches who are still looking for pitchers. Maybe we can talk about it at sports camp this summer." The recruiter made one last attempt to act like she cared. "Will we see you at camp?"

"It's already paid for, right? Then you'll see me." Lupe called out over her shoulder as she rushed up the last few benches to reach her brother. "David, how did you get here? It's so good to see you." They hugged each other, relieved to be together again. "Mama, how did this happen?"

"Good to see you, little sister, even if I still have one bum arm," David joked and held Lupe with his good arm. He gave her one of his old smiles. She thought that smile had been lost forever.

"Lupe, remember what I told you about the hospital bill being paid? Well, another odd thing happened." Mama leaned toward David. "Tell her, honey."

"I got a surprise visit from a bail bondsman early this morning," David said. "He came out of nowhere and paid my bail. He said he got a letter of credit from some hobby shop with my name on it."

"How's that possible? Did you sell something, maybe last month, before your accident?" Lupe knew this was the second time today she'd heard about a hobby shop. "What did the receipt say besides your name?"

"I have no idea what you two are talking about!" Mama said. "Who paid David's bail? Do you know?"

"The bondsman said the letter of credit was from a place called Sports Memorabilia Hobby Shop. Now, who do you know that could have done that?" David smiled at Lupe.

"Mr. Ramirez? Did he really do that?" Lupe remembered Mr. Ramirez's baseball collection.

"I wish I knew. Now I'm wondering about the hospital bill, too, poor man." Mama hung her head.

"David's out of jail, Mama. It's nothing to be sad about. We can just go to the Villa and thank Mr. Ramirez." Lupe remembered his closet packed with signed baseball caps and all his clippings, his plaque, and his poster of Roberto.

"No, we can't, Lupe." Mama reached out and squeezed Lupe's hand.

"Why not? He's not going anywhere." Lupe suddenly felt afraid.

"Mr. Ramirez had a stroke last night. An ambulance came while I was on my shift and took him away to the hospital." Mama let a tear roll down her cheek.

BOOK REPORT

TITLE: *The Geometry of Baseball*
SOURCE Mr. Dayneko's 8th Grade Math Class
CLASS: Geometry
TEACHER: Mr. Andrews
STUDENT: Lupe Lopez
DATE June 10, 1994

If you ask anyone the most important measure in baseball, they will tell you it's the number of wins versus losses for their favorite team. This paper is about the really important measures that are set up before any game can be won or lost. It is the true geometry of a baseball field, including the dimensions, angles, and some historical influences that have shaped the field.

Before I continue, I must tell you that I learned about an eighth grade math teacher who uses baseball to get his students interested in his class. Coach Collins referred me to Mr. Dayneko and he let me sit in on his classes.

If you were to close your eyes and imagine the baseball diamond, you might see the way bases are placed, the mound's angle, and the pitcher's pitch, and other elements that contribute to the unique geometry of a baseball diamond. But there are reasons for the structure of the diamond. In Mr. Dayneko's class I learned some fascinating truths behind the game's shape that caused me to challenge my assumptions and discover the true geometry of baseball.

If you are really using your imagination, you will see that there are a lot of differences between the infield and outfield dimensions, each with its own set of measures. The infield is constructed for swift plays and strategic maneuvers. Its measurements stick to strict standards. The bases form a diamond. They are precisely ninety feet apart. Inside that diamond, you find the pitcher's mound. It's higher than the rest of the infield to give the pitcher a strategic vantage. The sixty feet and six inches from the pitcher's mound to home plate is the space that gets the most attention when pitchers show off their skills.

The outfield, beyond the diamond, is a much bigger space but just as controlled and calculated to make the game a challenge. The distance to the outfield fence and the strategic placement of the bases in the infield reminds me of some of our most difficult geometry problems, when we are asked to judge distance and angles and arches. A player who can do this type of real-life geometry can really impress their teammates with their skill and strategy.

But one of the things that surprised me the most was that baseball fields and stadiums are not all alike. Teams have to adjust their playing strategies when they play teams in different locations.

I know it may be too late to get credit for this paper. I wish I'd known all this at the beginning of geometry class. I could have done a better job. It might even have improved my game. It really makes geometry interesting to me. Thanks, Mr. Dayneko!

CHAPTER 13

One week after graduation, a boring summer began. Life was quiet and miserable. There were no more softball games, and Lupe didn't know if she would ever have the chance to play again. Even worse, Lupe hated to admit it but Penny's ingenuity selling Mr. Ramirez's vintage baseball caps at the hobby shop paid for David's bail. Lupe even missed her daily visits to Villa Santa Barbara, a thing she never thought possible. Her volunteer hours were complete, and Mr. Ramirez was still in a rehabilitation hospital following his stroke.

Lupe felt guilty. What if he died? What if he was dead already? Would anyone remember him? She saw the notes for a paper she never turned in piled in the corner of her desk. Now she knew enough to go to the school library and ask the research librarian for help finding old news clips from the sports pages. She even took time to reread her notes about the stories Mr. Ramirez told her when he shared his baseball caps, jerseys, and clippings.

David was bored as he waited at home to appear at his court hearing. He wore an ankle monitor and had to stick near to the house. He and Lupe played cards, watched TV, and moped in their silent depression. Papa's old Chevy was finally released from impound. It was parked at the curb, a constant reminder of better days.

One Wednesday afternoon, David, who kept a close eye on the car, noticed a man appreciating it from across the road.

David called to his sister from the front porch.

"That old man wishes that was his car. Lupe, take a look at this guy." His voice was loud enough for the onlooker to hear him and raise his hand to wave and walk toward the house. "Oh God, get him out of here, Lupe."

"What? I'm watching *Law & Order* and it's almost over." Lupe hesitated to leave Papa's chair, where she was watching TV. "What do you want?"

"Come and take a look at this guy." David put down the matchbook he fiddled with to pass the time.

"Is that you, David? You look like your father, God rest his soul." The stranger approached the walkway leading to the front porch. Lupe stood out of sight, just inside the screen door. She recognized Uncle Waldo, Papa's brother, who hadn't visited the family since Papa's funeral over a year ago.

"It's *Tio* Waldo," Lupe whispered to David and wondered why their Holy Roller relation was finally making a visit. He and his family lived in the next county, but Mama and her brother-in-law were distant with one another.

"Is your mama here? I've got some great news." Uncle Waldo looked both ways before he came to the bottom of the steps.

"She's at work, *Tio*." Lupe opened the screen door and stepped out on the porch, curious about his great news. Mama would have wanted her to be more gracious, to give him a big hug and offer some lemonade, but she just didn't feel up to it.

"I saw you eyeballing Papa's Chevy. What brings you here?" David had no problem cutting to the chase.

"It's always been a beautiful automobile. Have you ever thought of selling it?" Uncle Waldo barely got the words out of his mouth when David got to his feet.

"No way in God's holy hell! What's your news?" David let him have it.

"Don't take the Lord's name in vain, young man. *Hijo de tu papa*—just like your old man."

Lupe stepped in front of David, not wanting the neighbors to see another disturbance on the front porch.

"Mama comes home between jobs, around six thirty. Can I get you some water?" Lupe forced herself to be friendly to the man who was never around when there was real trouble but was always full of advice.

"Thanks, Lupe. You're looking so much like your mother." Lupe gestured toward the second porch chair and kicked a warning toward her brother when her uncle's back was turned. She retrieved a glass of water and sat on the top step to hear his news. "I remember when you and my little Maria were girls, playing together with dolls and teacups."

"You do?" Lupe remembered her cousin, Maria, who'd loved to play the little mommy games that she'd never liked. The girls were the same age but attended different schools. It had been years since they were together. "Maria must have graduated this year, like me."

"Lupe plays softball. She's a great pitcher, going to the university this fall." David piped up, bragging about his sister, not wanting to be left out of the conversation. He knew her university dreams were all washed up.

"Softball? Well, well. That's something I never expected. I thought you were the athlete in the family, David."

"Still am." David lied again and crossed his legs to hide his ankle monitor. "So what's your news?"

"Great news! The Lord has blessed us. Maria is getting married, and we want you all to attend the ceremony." Uncle Waldo's joy sounded forced.

"Married? She just graduated from high school." Lupe couldn't help blurting this out.

"Well, actually, she'll do that later, take an exam or something to finish. She is in love, and we are glad he's such a wonderful young man. Roger Hamilton. He's our pastor's son and plans to go into the ministry, like his dad."

"Are you talking about Roger Hamilton from Cleveland High? I played against him in high school." David looked suspicious.

"Yes. You knew him before you dropped out? He's a fine young Christian athlete." *Tio* Waldo took a jab at David, and then spoke more enthusiastically about his future son-in-law than he had about his own daughter, *prima* Maria.

"I only knew him by reputation." David's voice was low.

"Well, Mama will be happy to hear this. When is the wedding?" Lupe knew her mama would hold this over her head. She always compared her with Maria. She wanted to know why Lupe never dressed up, seldom went out with boys, and didn't act more like a lady.

"July 4; it's a red, white, and blue wedding. As long as there are fireworks, we thought we would take advantage of the celebration. It's at our church, of course, Camino de la Luz, three o'clock, then a barbecue reception afterward."

"So soon." Lupe tried to imagine how Maria could make such a big decision while she was still so young.

"I get it, kind of a firecracker theme, eh?" David had a sneer on his face.

"I have to rush off, kids. Tell your mama, and I certainly hope you can all come. Don't worry about bringing a gift. Pastor

Hamilton and his wife are giving the new couple everything they need to get started."

There was no handshake for David and no hug for Lupe. Uncle Waldo seemed to be in a big hurry to be on his way. He did slow down to pat the hood of the Chevy as he passed, and Lupe heard her brother make a low growl.

"Just wait till Mama hears about this," Lupe muttered.

"He certainly hopes we can all attend." David rubbed his ankle below the restraining bracelet.

"Hello! Where are you two?" Mama arrived two hours later, carrying a paper plate of stale cookies covered with plastic wrap. "I have sweets and news to share." She sometimes brought home leftovers from the Villa.

Lupe and David were watching a Dodger's game on TV. They were deep into analyzing the starting lineup of players when Mama arrived.

"We already got the news. Maria is getting married," David called out over his shoulder. "What kind of sweets?"

"There you are. Maria what? Sugar cookies, store bought." Mama placed the paper plate between her teenagers, who were glued to the baseball game. "Welcome home, mommy. Thank you for the sweets and for working all day and night to keep us fed." She mocked her children and headed for the shower.

"Thanks, Mama." When her mother showered between jobs, it was the signal for Lupe to get dinner started for the three of them. "*Tio* Waldo was here." The shower water was running, and Mama didn't respond. Lupe stepped into the kitchen to retrieve two bowls, eggs, tortillas, and salsa from the secondhand refrigerator. Scrambled eggs with beans and rice were a standard weeknight meal shared by the family.

"What did you say about your long-lost uncle?" Mama's hair was still wet when the Dodger's game was finally over and they all sat around the table. "David, move that glove."

"First, tell us your news." Lupe was in no hurry to tell Mama about Maria's wedding.

"I am being promoted and getting a raise!" Mama held up her water glass, making a toast. "Can you believe it? It's another miracle, thanks to your Mr. Ramirez, Lupe."

"Isn't he still in rehab?" David had never taken the time to visit his benefactor and thank him for paying his bail.

"He is, and waiting for a visit from both of you. *Sin verguenza*—shame on you. I visited him myself, and he requested that I be promoted to be his caregiver when he returns to the Villa." Mama sat up straight and pushed back her shoulders with pride. "They agreed. My training starts tomorrow. This is my last night of doing the laundry for the Villa."

"And they are giving you more money? They sure couldn't give you any less." David stuffed his face with the burrito he rolled with his eggs and beans.

"That's great, Mom. I never expected that Mr. Ramirez would do so much for us." Lupe recalled her repulsion when she first met the old man in the wheelchair.

"We never know where our blessings will come from, Lupe." Mom tore a piece of tortilla and daintily scooped up a bit of rice.

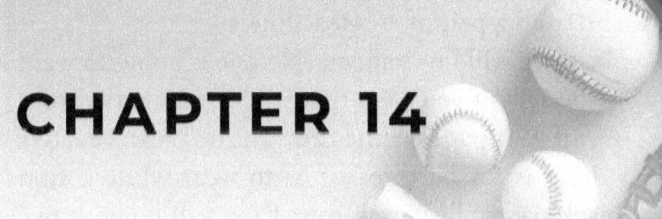

CHAPTER 14

There were three things that Lupe did not look forward to: her cousin's wedding, David's court hearing, and visiting Mr. Ramirez. Even thinking of the softball camp that she once looked forward to now drained her energy. Maybe because she knew she would have to see Penny.

The summer was hotter than usual. David was grouchy every day for one reason or another. He did have permission to leave the house for Cousin Maria's wedding in the next county.

The wedding was just one week away. Softball camp at the university began the Monday following the wedding. That same week David's court hearing was scheduled. And finally, it was the same week Mr. Ramirez would return to Villa Santa Barbara. Mama said his stroke left his left arm frozen and his speech slurred.

"Show me what you are going to wear to your cousin's wedding." Mama wanted the family to make a good impression in front of her brother-in-law and his church friends. "No, you are not wearing that skimpy sundress, Lupe." There was no money for a new dress.

"It's going to be hot as blazes on the Fourth of July, Mama. No one will be looking at us anyway. We'll be strangers to the other guests—the heathen cousins." David selected a Santana T-shirt and a pair of creased chinos.

"Of course, we will be strangers. No one is going to want to know us, especially if you wear that wild-eyed man on your chest. Get one of your papa's white dress shirts; Lupe, you, too. The easiest thing is for all three of us to wear white cotton shirts over black pants. That way your Papa will be with us." Lupe seldom witnessed her mama being so nervous, but this was the first family event they were going to attend since Papa had died. And to make matters worse, it was with the Protestant branch of the family.

The evangelical Camino de la Luz church where Uncle Waldo and his family had "come to Jesus" was a simple, wood-frame building set back from the street by a broad dry lawn. Today the yard was set with folding tables and chairs in preparation for the barbecue reception following the church wedding.

"This is not really a church," Mama whispered to Lupe when they were seated in the back pew. "They don't even have Jesus on that cross or any statues of the saints." She spoke in Spanish, and Lupe was certain that no one around them could understand her criticisms.

The only familiar part of the ceremony was the wedding march music. It was piped in from some fuzzy recording. It began when Maria and her father stood at the back of the church ready to walk down the aisle. Everyone turned to look at Maria's dress, which was a series of bright white ruffles from her neck down to her ankles. Lupe thought she resembled a flocked Christmas tree. David looked his cousin over as she wobbled down the aisle. Lupe knew what David was thinking. "She's a knocked-up high school dropout," he had assured her. Despite the plain church and the unflattering dress, Mama dabbed her eyes with a tissue and continued to whisper in Spanish.

"*Fijate mija*—think, Lupe." She smiled in spite of herself. "Someday it will be your turn, and I will be so proud."

This was one of Mama's dreams. Her maternal wishes came out in small ways. She was not bossy or outspoken like some mothers. Lupe heard other women ragging on their daughters in public. Sometimes she heard mother/daughter arguments on the bus or in a department store. Her mama was much more subtle but she had the same traditional ideas of how Lupe's future should unfold.

When Mom said, "You really have nice eyes," she was actually telling Lupe to highlight them with makeup. If she said, "Mona Vasquez has a handsome son," she was sending the message: "You ought to be going out with him."

Most often her comments were about housekeeping or Lupe's lack thereof. She'd say, "Someday you'll know how important it is to sweep the kitchen floor each night, to fry an egg without breaking the yolk, to separate the laundry into white and dark loads."

Lupe imagined her mama envisioning her "someday" as a housekeeper—an orderly, tidy wife and mother who made her husband and maybe a mother-in-law—*Oh, God help me!*—proud and happy. That was the furthest thing from Lupe's dreams.

Lupe forced herself to pay attention to the wedding service. All she could think of was the bride, committing herself for a lifetime. Mama did it, and so had every other woman in the family. It seemed to be such a huge gamble. Lupe had no idea what was coming next in her life. Maybe sports camp would open up new possibilities. If not, how else was she ever going to make Mama proud?

The reception was equally plain. The barbecues made the area smoky. The folding tables and chairs were hot as blazes and unstable on the lawn, which was full of gopher holes. Since Lupe, David, and Mama were dressed in Papa's white shirts and black pants, the other guests kept turning to them with their empty plates and glasses, mistaking them for hired servers. Mama complied, as a member of the family would, until David held her down to one spot.

"Can't we go now?" David whined. They were strangers among all the church attendees.

"Not yet," Mama said. "We'll wait until after the toast. Then Maria and her papa will have the first dance. That will be nice."

But there was no champagne toast or alcohol of any type. No live music or dancing. Instead, a series of balding men gave long prayers for the newlyweds, holding plastic cups of lemonade aloft. The groom's father, Pastor Hamilton, made the longest remarks, welcoming everyone to attend his church services the following morning and recognizing every member of the family except Mama, David, and Lupe.

Santa Barbara Sporting News

A Roll Call from Our Local Teams

Summer 1994

Former Athlete Trains for
Ministry and Marriage

Former Athlete-of-the-Year, Roger Hamilton, Cleveland High School class of 1993, has announced professional and personal plans. Hamilton, previously known as our Home Run King, takes on new opportunities and challenges as he continues to support our community.

A marriage announcement, recently spotted in the local news, declared Roger Hamilton intends to wed Maria Lopez this July 4 at the Camino de la Luz church. The marriage will be conducted by the groom's father, Pastor Jake Hamilton. Apparently, Roger intends to follow in his father's footsteps as the couple plans to move to Dallas, Texas, where he will study at the theological seminary. All of us at *Sporting News* wish the newlyweds a heavenly home run!

CHAPTER 15

The week following Cousin Maria's wedding, Lupe retrieved the letter admitting her to the week-long summer sports camp from a cluttered shelf in her room at home. She already knew it was to take place at the local university and that it included free tuition, room, board, and some complimentary sports equipment. When she'd first received the invitation months ago, she'd been thrilled. The softball recruiter told Lupe that she would be selected by a top school and awarded a full scholarship to begin her college career.

Now that hope had vanished. Her friendship with Penny, her teammate and catcher, was over, too. Their season had ended badly. Even though the recruiter went on to court more successful players, she assured Lupe that she would still be welcomed at the summer camp. So Lupe packed a bag. It was a brown grocery bag. Beyond her backpack, she didn't have a suitcase or even a duffel bag. When she traveled for her high school away games, it never included an overnight stay. Hotels were not in the school budget, so the exhausted players rode their bus home overnight. The last time she spent the night away from home was when she and her cousin Maria were eight years old. Mama and Papa had left Lupe and David with Uncle Waldo's family for a long weekend. *That must have been when I was forced to play with Maria's stupid dolls*, Lupe thought.

"*Adelante*—hurry up. You are going to miss your bus to the university." Mama tucked a few treats wrapped in foil into Lupe's brown bag.

"I still don't see why David can't drive me to the campus." Lupe dragged her feet walking to the front door. "I bet no one else going to camp has to catch a six-thirty bus." The so-called University Express bus would get her to the campus in order to check in at camp by 8:00 a.m.

"You know your brother's court hearing is today. He's got to be on time, showered, shaved, and on his best behavior. I wish you could be with us." Mama followed Lupe to the bus stop at the end of the block. "I can't believe you will be gone all week. The first week I won't be working the midnight laundry shift at the Villa. What am I going to do without you?"

"Try *Law & Order*; it's always on and they never lose a case." Lupe wanted to make Mama laugh and hoped the court hearing for David would go well. "I'll call you tonight at eight."

When Lupe arrived at the university campus, she didn't have to ask for directions to the baseball field. Cars were backed up on the narrow road. Each one held a young player, usually accompanied by her parents. Some were already unloading several pieces of matched luggage. Mothers or fathers, sometimes both, pressed cash into their daughters' hands. Lupe even saw some girls being handed credit cards. Were they going to play ball this week, or were they here to shop at the university village stores? She clutched her brown bag and bus pass, hoping no one would notice her.

"High school graduates here. Underclass students go to the left." An older student with a plastic name badge herded the arriving players into two separate dormitories. Lupe realized it was the first time she ever identified herself as a high school graduate. She walked to the right, as instructed, with her eyes locked on a bright, new duffel bag with the words University Sports Camp on it, hanging from the arm of the girl in front of her.

"Nice bag," she commented out loud before she could stop herself. To her relief, the girl who turned to respond looked a lot like her.

"Did you get yours? They are giving them away at registration with a lot of other cool stuff." The girl's eyes slid down to Lupe's brown paper bag. "I can show you where. My name is Amelia."

"Could you? That would be great." Lupe let go of the long breath she had been holding since she'd gotten off the bus. She was actually able to smile at this girl. "Lupe. Pitcher. I can get rid of this old thing." She lifted the bag she kept hidden from everyone else and followed Amelia across a crunchy patch of lawn toward a long table piled high with bags, jerseys, socks, and other team gear.

"You're a pitcher? No way!" Amelia measured her stride to match Lupe's and started a conversation as they walked. "I play shortstop; my fastball wasn't fast enough to make the cut." There was a tall girl in front of them when they reached the registration table.

"No, thank you, I don't want any of the free stuff. I have my own things," the girl ahead of them said. "Just give me the badge."

"I'll take her stuff if she doesn't want it." Amelia was joking.

"It looks like you already have your free stuff," the woman monitoring the table responded to her. "Next."

"This is my friend Lupe, a pitcher." Lupe looked between Amelia and the woman, and then held out her invitation letter from the recruiter. The woman studied the letter. Her eyebrows rose when she read the date and signature.

"Oh, an early recruit. Welcome." She glanced back at the letter. "Lupe Lopez. I'm Coach Ferguson from City College." She proceeded to open a new duffel and load in two of everything on the table to Lupe's amazement. "Let me know if you need anything else."

"Thanks a lot." Lupe crumbled her brown bag into the remaining space in the official sports camp bag. "Can I ask you, is Penny Williams on your list?"

"She's on the list but hasn't checked in yet. Do you know her?"

"Kind of." Lupe turned to follow Amelia toward the dormitory assignments.

For two days, the time was filled with exercise stations, huge group meals in a crowded dining hall, and a few pep talk lectures in the early evening. Lupe was exhausted by the end of the day. She crawled into bed as soon as possible after a brief call to Mama.

"Yes, I'm okay. How was the court hearing?" Lupe asked. "Boring? Didn't they get to David's case? Tomorrow?"

Amelia was assigned to a different room, and the girls didn't see each other until the second afternoon when teams were assigned and the first practice game was scheduled. Nervous about her pitching performance, Lupe silently prayed, "Let Amelia be on my team, please." *What if that happened and then she saw Penny?*

"Okay, athletes, if you think you are tired now, just wait until we play three days of doubleheaders." The camp participants sat on the field and released a collective groan. The camp director continued. "Come on. That's why you're here, right?"

She wore a tiny lapel microphone that amplified her words to the one hundred assembled players.

Lupe and Amelia found each other and sat side by side.

"Maybe you came for the pool parties or for our very special guest speaker on Friday night," the director said. "If you have never heard gold medalist Lisa Fernandez speak, you are in for a big treat. She's a California player, too, and you won't want to miss it."

At the mention of Lisa Fernandez, Lupe and Amelia jumped to their feet and cheered, as did many of the participants.

"That's why I'm here," Amelia grinned, her clapping hands held high above her head.

"I had no idea. I can't believe it! Fernandez here, in person?" Lupe, eyes wide, kept clapping after many of the girls sat down. "Wait till I tell my brother."

"Your brother—does he play?" This was the first time the girls had a chance to talk about themselves beyond their positions on the field.

"He did. He's kind of out with an injury now." Lupe didn't tell the entire truth. "But he's the one who taught me when I was a kid."

"Okay, listen up." The camp director returned to her announcements. "Expect one hundred players, six teams, and three fields in motion for the next three days." There was more groaning from some players and cheers from others. "Six coaches are standing around the perimeter. Each holds a colored card. Listen for your name and team color, then move your butts to that coach and get ready to play."

Lupe and Amelia were both named to the blue team. The coach holding the blue card was the woman from the registration table, Coach Ferguson.

"Her again." Amelia grinned, and they got in line with their team.

The competition among the teams during three days of doubleheaders was fierce. Lupe's performance was even but average compared with the speed of the other pitchers on the blue team, and the other teams as well. The coaches gave the players equal time in their positions. Lupe's bench time in the dugout gave her plenty of time to observe other players. *Still no sign of Penny.* It also kept her from being totally exhausted. As usual, there was a lot of chatter in the dugout.

"Claremont, Santa Clara, San Diego." The girls shared their university plans with one another. Most of the schools Lupe had never heard of. She had nothing to say and pretended to be studying the game in action.

"What do you think?" Coach Ferguson took a break to sit next to her. "Amelia's pretty good at shortstop, isn't she?" The coach didn't talk to many players during the game except to give them playing instruction. "She's mine, you know."

"Yours?" Lupe turned to speak directly to Ferguson.

"She's playing for my team, the City College Gauchos, this fall. Hopefully, I have her for two years. It's a smart move."

"It sounds like everyone in this dugout is going to big universities. What makes it so smart?" Lupe had been so intent on getting a scholarship with her friend Penny during high school that she'd never taken notice of possibilities with other schools. When her high school grades had fallen below the required 3.5 grade point average and Penny had made plans to go to Irvine, Lupe had no alternate plans in place. "I mean, yeah, Amelia looks really good out there." Lupe didn't mean to insult the City College coach.

"Are you the first, Lupe?" Coach Ferguson dropped her voice a little. "I mean the first in your family to play, to go to college? Lots of my players are new to the system."

How had she known? Since that first day, Lupe sensed that this coach had been watching her. It was a little creepy, like the feeling that Roberto Clemente's ghost would pop out of nowhere and start talking to her.

"Well, my brother plays, but he didn't finish high school. So that makes me the first."

By Friday night, the evening of the pool party and the guest lecture by Lisa Fernandez, Lupe felt like she had made more friends than she ever imagined having. The blue team bonded during their three doubleheaders, even though their wins weren't at the top of the chart. Lupe became acquainted with the pitchers on the other five teams, and they were already talking about attending special pitching clinics at the end of the summer. With all its shortcomings, she had not realized how much she missed her high school team after graduation. The fun and competitive action brought her to life and distracted her from worrying about her family and their financial struggles.

"Here's my phone number in case I forget before we leave, Lupe. We've got to stay in touch." Amelia extended a scrap of paper in her direction. The thought of leaving the camp environment depressed Lupe.

"You're going to City College right here in town, aren't you? You know, I live here." Lupe took the paper and pushed it down in her pocket. Would Amelia really want to stay in touch?

"What? You haven't said a word about where you live or your family other than it was your brother who taught you to play." Amelia poked Lupe in the ribs. "Ms. Mysterious Pitcher,

Lupe Lopez. Why didn't we meet earlier during the high school season?"

"Ladies. Athletes. I'm calling you ladies because I want you to act like it and welcome our special guest, the gold medal winner for Team USA, the fantastic native Californian, Lisa Fernandez!" Lupe jerked around toward the director's voice, hardly believing she was about to see and hear her shero speak in person.

It was an unforgettable night. Sure, the crowd went crazy when Lisa Fernandez stepped onto the stage and waved her cap above her head, but she looked completely normal, like a sister or another relative. She was taller and a little older than Lupe, but when she began to talk it seemed like they had known each other all their lives. She spoke about her victories and her setbacks. She admitted her self-doubts and awkward moments, on and off the field, with other professional players, and even with men. When she did this her eyes seemed to lock on Lupe. Lupe's mind traveled all the way from *Poor me, I don't know what I'm going to do in the future to, if Lisa can do it, so can I. I'm going to take the next step, whatever it is, and keep on pitching!* The crowd cheered her speech, and a chant began to spread among the players.

"Always do your best. Make it happen," Lisa said. Lupe and Amelia screamed side by side.

The next morning Lupe lingered, knowing she would miss the first bus to the terminal closest to her house. She wanted to give Amelia one last high five and her phone number. She hoped Amelia would not ask about where she lived.

"Do you have a ride? What part of town do you live in? My mom can load up your stuff." Amelia headed to the curb with two sports camp duffel bags, one slung over each shoulder.

"No. I've got a ride, thanks." Lupe wanted to be polite without mentioning her neighborhood to Amelia.

"I see you somehow managed to get a second duffel, young lady." Coach Ferguson approached and tugged on one of Amelia's bags. "You're going to have to work extra hard in two weeks to pay that off. Here's the schedule." She handed Amelia a laminated page and turned to Lupe, holding a large manila envelope. "Too bad you can't join us for the special clinics. It's only for registered freshmen."

"Geez, Coach, you've seen what a good arm she has. Can't you make an exception?" Amelia put down her bags and studied the laminated clinic schedule.

"That's okay; I'm sure I'll be busy." Lupe longed to get more playing time. She stood up straight with a forced smile.

"Well, there's one way you could come." Coach Ferguson's voice slowed down, and Lupe thought she saw her wink at Amelia. "This envelope contains a City College application and a letter of recommendation from me that you can turn in to the college admissions office. We'd love to have you join us, no matter what other offers you have on the table."

"Well, I don't know." Lupe strung out her reply as long as she could, not wanting to lie to the coach.

"I promise you will get lots of playing time if you keep working as hard as you have this week." The coach leaned over to see under Lupe's visor, which hung down. "A lot of players don't realize they can do two years at City College for free and get an automatic transfer to a four-year school when they graduate."

"It's a really good deal, Lupe," Amelia chimed in. Lupe wondered, *did she and Coach plan this all along?*

"But it's almost August. It's too late." Lupe couldn't believe she could be this lucky. She automatically looked around to see if Roberto Clemente's ghost was nearby. "Just fill this in? Really, that's all?" Lupe kept expecting a letdown.

Amelia danced around with her hands up and repeated Lisa Fernandez's chant from last night.

"Remember, always do your best. Make it happen." They all laughed.

"It's late; you're right. Do you have some sample writing you can include with the application?" Coach Ferguson asked.

"I have some research notes on an old baseball recruiter I know," Lupe said with some hesitation.

"That's perfect. Send me a copy," Coach Ferguson said. "Take all that to the City College admissions office as soon as you can. Here, take this clinic schedule and talk about it with your family." Coach Ferguson handed her the laminated schedule and turned to go. "I've got to head out, ladies. I hope to see you both soon." She took a few steps and turned back. "Lupe, it will make your mom proud. Believe me."

As the coach walked away Lupe noticed the name on the back of her jersey: "Clemente," it read.

Santa Barbara Sporting News

A Roll Call from Our Local Teams

Summer 1994

Sports Camp Special Speaker Lisa Fernandez

Attendees at this summer's university sports camp were treated to a special speaker, all-American softball star Lisa Fernandez.

In 1990, Fernandez won a gold medal at the International Softball Federation (ISF) World Championship. Among her accomplishments are the following: 1991 gold medal at the Pan American Games, 1994 gold medals at ISF World School Championship, 1991 Pan-Am Olympic Qualifier, and 1992 Sportswoman of the Year. Her remarks inspired and motivated the young athletes.

Her theme was loud and clear: "The team with the best athletes doesn't usually win. It's the team with the athletes who play best together."

Fernandez starred both on the field and at the plate for the UCLA Bruins from 1990 to 1993 and was two-time national champion and four-time first team all-American.

An Application to Santa Barbara City College

Applicant: Lupe Lopez, 674 Pine Street, Santa Barbara, CA
Sponsor: Coach Ferguson, Women's softball team, SBCC athletic department
Note: Coach Ferguson asked me to turn in this writing sample with my application.
TITLE: Luis Olmo
SOURCE: Newspaper Archives on American Baseball
DATE: August 15, 1994

NOTE: This paper was written just before my high school graduation with notes from two sources. The first is a friend of mine, Mr. Raul Ramirez, a former National League scout and recruiter. The second was my high school library, with the help of our research librarian. We found what I was looking for. I wanted to know if Mr. Ramirez, whom I met a Villa Santa Barbara, was really who he said he was. I found him in an article about Luis Olmo, another very famous recruiter.

I would have done a lot more papers if I had known earlier about how research librarians can help students find old newspapers and sports statistics. Even though I just graduated, I think teachers should tell more students about this. I have learned that a person can find information on anything that interests them, even if it's just baseball!

The title of this book report says it is about Luis Olmo, a Puerto Rican player who was said to have recruited Roberto Clemente to the National League.

To be absolutely honest, it could also be about Rafael Avila, a Dominican who directed a major league training camp for Latin American players. But this report is truly about a man named Raul Ramirez, whom I discovered as part of my community service requirement hours at Villa Santa Barbara.

Mr. Ramirez had a mini baseball museum in his room with news clippings, signed balls, caps, and jerseys from the top Latin American players over the last fifty years. He had all this stuff because he was the recruiter for Major League Baseball throughout Latin America. He told me that he was the one who recruited Roberto Clemente, and I believe him. He also told me that he started the famous baseball academy in the Dominican Republic (DR) and helped many players get ready to play in the US. I believe him about that, too. He has pictures of the young players and the first diamonds that they played on in camp.

"The DR's first professional league was founded in 1890. In the fifty years since the first Dominican debuted in Major League Baseball in 1956, over 400 players from the nation have played in the league." New York Times, Sports Section, May 15, 1985

I looked all this up with Mr. Ramirez and found out that all thirty big league teams have academies. As far as history goes, those academies have added an average of $90 million a year to the local economies. The DR and other Caribbean countries that have these baseball camps are some of the poorest places in the world. So baseball changes history.

I'm going to write to the New York Times and tell them that they have to add more about Raul

Ramirez to their reports. I can share his pictures and other stuff so he gets the credit for all he has done. I'm so glad I had to do my community service and was assigned to Villa Santa Barbara, where I met this sports hero and some other nice people, whom I now call my friends.

CHAPTER 16

"Going to the local city college is a waste; it's just like an extension of high school." Lupe had heard this expressed many times, usually from kids who were heading to large universities far from home for their freshman year.

However, city college was completely different from Lupe's high school experience. The campus looked different, felt different, and was a fresh start for her life as a player and as a student. The classrooms were spread across two hilltops overlooking the Pacific Ocean and seemed more like a resort hotel than a school. Many students looked similar to Lupe—dark hair, eyes, and skin, and about her size, too. The majority of the students seemed to have some ethnic or racial identities different from most of the kids Lupe had in her high school classes. There were older students, too—really old. She wondered if these people, many with gray hair, were starting their lives all over again. They were smart, never afraid to speak up in class.

Even though she enjoyed the green lawns and ocean views, Lupe felt city college was kind of overwhelming. Facing a crowd of new teachers and students at the city college was an entirely new experience. Who were all these people inhabiting the campus just outside of Lupe's lifelong neighborhood?

There were so many unfamiliar faces, accents, and personalities. The annoying, frivolous high school students she once knew must have enrolled at other campuses.

The city college students looked and sounded much more serious. They lugged around heavy books and read actual newspapers, not just party flyers and merchandise pamphlets. They all seemed to have work schedules that meshed with their time on campus attending classes and studying in the library.

The faculty had a different look, too. They seemed to be older than her high school teachers. They dressed much more carelessly; it was a kind of frumpy look. Even though they looked less put together, they somehow acted much more confident. They spoke as if they were sure of their subject matter and dead serious. Lupe knew she had to step up her own study skills. She noticed that these professors were much less tolerant of students who arrived at class without having done their homework.

In her first month attending this new school she even witnessed confrontations in the classroom. They were not always student arguments, but actual debates between students and the teachers, especially those who liked to be called professor, or even doctor!

Unfortunately, half the players on the softball team held a poor opinion of the school, as if it was a low-budget version of a real college experience or just a stepping stone in their sports career. Coach Ferguson put a quick end to that.

"I want everyone to get a dollar out of your backpack, right now. I mean it. If I hear anyone saying, 'It's just city college,' you owe me that dollar. If I notice anyone who seems to think that we will automatically lose our games against large university teams, you owe me that dollar. I'm here to win and give you more playing time in competitive games than any of your fancy-pants friends who are freshmen at some big four-year university. They will only be warming the university bench while you're batting in the city college lineup. Trust me on this."

Lupe and Amelia found out right away what a perfectly matched pair they were. Lupe pitched and Amelia played shortstop. They had a chemistry that players sometimes take years to develop. Amelia could read what pitch Lupe was going to deliver and anticipate how the batter would respond.

There was one member of the team, at second base, who messed up more plays than anyone, Skippy Li. She was one of the players who had a low opinion of the school and thought she should be at some higher-ranking college. She was often out of position and had an annoying habit that earned her the nickname "Skippy." For every ground ball she captured in her glove, she took a short skip before releasing her throw. Every time she caught a ball that bounced in the infield, her annoying skip preceded her throw. It drove Lupe crazy.

"Why does she do that? Does she think she's being cute?" Lupe complained to Amelia on more than one occasion until one day she erupted during a game.

"Open those eyes, Li!" The minute she said it she knew there would be trouble. It was just an expression and nothing about her eyes, which were definitely almond shaped. Skippy began to scream at Lupe. Jenny Wong, in right field, joined her at the baseline. Amelia ran to stand between Lupe and the other two girls. Immediately all the players on the team took sides.

"Get it together, Coach." The umpire halted play, waving in Coach Ferguson, who removed Lupe from the game and replaced her with another pitcher.

"You've seen what she does, Coach. She never gets the ball to first on time. All because of that stupid skip." Lupe sulked on the bench.

"What did you call me?" Ferguson snapped back at Lupe.

"What do you mean? I only called you Coach."

"Exactly, I am the coach. You are the pitcher—whenever I choose to put you in the game." Coach Ferguson took a deep breath and shook her head from side to side. "I know her skip slows us down. I've talked to her about it. That's my job, Lupe, not yours. Play your position."

It sounded easier than it was. Lupe's pitches were getting faster and more accurate, but what did it matter if other players weren't doing their best? That was one of the toughest lessons she had to learn in her freshman year at City College: holding her temper and playing her own position.

Santa Barbara Sporting News

A Roll Call from Our Local Teams

Spring 1995

City College Hosts University Farm Team

New regulations in the state of California's student transfer policies create the perfect conditions for a university farm team at SBCC and all state community colleges.

"We have always been proud of our players and the effort they bring to our community college teams. Under the new state rules we have the opportunity to ensure their successful transfer into our four-year university system once student athletes complete all requirements for their AA degree at SBCC." Coach Ferguson is enthusiastic about the changes.

In addition to the automatic transfer policy and the reasonable rates for student tuition at the community college, administrators report a greater diversity among attendees is evident. Students from various ethnic, racial, and economic backgrounds are all welcomed at SBCC.

CHAPTER 17

During registration for her sophomore year, a class appeared on her schedule that Lupe had not selected: Interpersonal Communications and Group Dynamics.

"How did this get here?" Lupe complained to the registrar. "It's a mistake."

"No, it fulfills your language requirement for your Associate of Arts degree."

"I tested out of that with Spanish." Lupe held her finger on the class title. "I don't need this class."

"Would you prefer French or German?" the registrar asked.

"That's crazy. Take it off the schedule, please." Lupe didn't think she was being rude, but the registrar drew back away from her.

"Can't get into a class?" One of the campus security guards walked up behind her. "It can be frustrating. Just calm down, young lady." Now everyone in line to register was looking at Lupe like she was some kind of troublemaker.

"I can't drop a class? How ridiculous is that?" Lupe knew how to build her own schedule. She felt embarrassed but couldn't help getting upset over this mistake.

"Okay, look. The semester doesn't start for weeks." The security guard spoke to her in slow, measured words. He was used to dealing with frustrated students. "Leave the class on your registration and drop it the first week of the term." Lupe looked up at this broad-shouldered guard and immediately recognized him as one of David's former classmates.

"Aren't you Chuck Romo? Didn't you play for the Dons? My brother, David Lopez, was on that team."

"Yeah, I remember David. Are we okay here"—he looked down at her registration card—"Lupe?" She nodded and got control of her temper immediately. As Romo turned to walk away, he asked, "What happened to David? Where is he?"

Lupe didn't think David would want her to share his recent history even though he was out of his ankle cuff now and doing volunteer work, he was still on probation.

The registrar took Lupe's signed card without speaking to her again. She did call out to the guard in a flirty voice, "Thanks, Chuck!"

"Just because you know what you are thinking doesn't mean anyone else understands your thoughts," the communications teacher lectured on the first day of class. "And just because you've told someone about your feelings doesn't mean they actually understand how you feel."

Well, what's the use, then? Lupe considered the idea of engaging in conversation rather than getting mad or running away. She learned it was not always the best strategy to get upset. After class she tried out the teacher's suggestions on the baseball field.

"Skipper, I think you could throw more runners out at first if you stopped skipping before you released the ball." Lupe tried to recuperate from her earlier comments to Skipper. But the result was the same.

"Who made you the coach?" Skipper snapped back at her. "You're just jealous about my personal style of play. Admit it."

"No, I just think we could win more games if we were all a little faster, myself included." It was her first attempt to improve her communication style. She decided she had better stay in the communications class.

Little by little, her team conversations improved. The players became more of a unit, and then won a few more games. After three weeks Coach Ferguson commented on Lupe's efforts.

"Nicely done, Lupe. Maybe we should be calling you Coach," Ferguson said to her after a game.

"What? Me?" Lupe bent over to dry her hair with a towel after pulling on her street clothes. "Oh, you mean Skipper. The longer she plays, the better she gets."

"One of my baseball heroes said, 'It's not the best players who win games, it's the teams that know how to play together that win games.' I think it's the way you've been talking to her and the rest of the team that makes us play better."

"It sounds like something that Roberto Clemente would say," Lupe said.

"Exactly! He loved to coach kids like the ones running around at the East Side Field," Coach Ferguson said. "They need that same type of encouragement."

He's still there, Lupe wanted to say. But instead she said, "My brother volunteers with the East Side kids and tells some pretty funny stories about the teams."

"Did you know you could get education course credits by coaching at that field?" Ferguson looked around at the few players left in the locker room. "Well, not just coaching. You'd have to learn how to do a lesson plan and write up some observations about the kids. Do you have any interest in that?"

"Actual credits? I do need another class to finish my two years and transfer to the university. I never thought about taking an education class or teaching."

CHAPTER 18

After that conversation Lupe made a point of going back to the same registrar she had complained to about the communications class. She apologized and told her how effective what she had been learning was with the team. Then she asked for help getting registered for credit to coach the kids at the East Side Field. The woman was so impressed that she smoothed the way for the new course credits and introduced Lupe to the education professor.

"I'm glad to meet you, Lupe. I don't remember seeing you in any of our education classes," Dr. Phillips said. "I understand you hope to get credit for coaching a kids' softball team."

"That's right. I'm a pitcher." Lupe pressed her lips together and held her breath.

"Did you bring your lesson plans for me to approve?" Dr. Phillips moved away from Lupe toward her desk. She held out her hand, expecting Lupe to hand her something.

"Well, not really. I've never done that." Lupe exhaled. What could she say? "I'm here to learn. Is there a book or something?" Some of the other students were overhearing the conversation. Lupe watched the rest of the class out of the corner of her eye.

Dr. Phillips glanced up at the ceiling, her patience obviously running thin. "Shirley, do you have a copy of the lesson plan framework in your notebook?"

"No, just one of the lesson plans, that's all." A student near Lupe spoke up. She ripped a page from her binder and held it out. "Is this what you want?"

"You can read this, can't you, Ms. Pitcher?" The rest of the girls in the class shifted around. "Take this and bring me six weeks of plans. Then I'll sign off on your registration, and you can start coaching.

"Six weeks? I start coaching tomorrow." Lupe took the paper and moved toward the door. This was not going to be as easy as she had hoped. Plus she felt humiliated in front of this class of strangers. She forced herself to slow down. "Thanks. I'll do this," she managed to say before she closed the door behind her.

When Lupe returned home, she was craving some peace and quiet. She went right out to the backyard to have a talk with Shelly. During the winter months, Shelly covered herself up in her backyard sandbox. Lupe actually missed seeing her. She sat on the edge of the box and talked to the tortoise.

"Did you have a good day, Shelly?" Lupe stared at the sandbox. "It always seems so peaceful out here." Lupe glanced around her familiar backyard. "You wouldn't believe all the stuff I deal with in my classes and even during practice with my own teammates. We're all supposed to be on the same team. Every day our coach pushes us so hard at practice. I just don't get why some people act the way they do. You're lucky, all alone in your own space all day."

Later that evening, Lupe explained everything that had happened at school to David, but he was more interested in hearing about his old buddy, Romo, the security guard.

"I remember Romo. He was a big deal on the field. The last I heard he was heading to Miami to play for a feeder school for Tampa. What's he doing playing cop games at City College?" David was getting dressed to do his probation volunteer hours at the East Side Field. He slid into his old baseball uniform, looking a lot like Lupe remembered him from his high school days.

"Well, he might say the same thing about you, Mr. East Side Coach. Things don't always turn out the way we plan them." She was relieved that David's year-long probation included community service hours at the ballpark. Again, it seemed like someone was looking out for him.

"Yeah, like Papa dying so young. What a bad break that was for all of us." David turned away from Lupe but she guessed that he was fighting off tears. "At least he'd be glad that we are both playing ball."

"I can't coach until I do these stupid lesson plans. Have you ever done one?"

"I thought you were going to coach, not teach." He reached for his cap. "Just come meet the kids today."

"I guess I could visit before I start coaching. But I really need to figure out how to do softball lesson plans." Lupe slipped off her jacket and pulled a jersey over her shirt. "By the way, did I tell you our shortstop really wants to meet you?"

"Yeah, right, your loser brother. I haven't talked with a girl since I got beaten up." David rubbed his pitching arm and headed for the Chevy. "I'll look at that paper when we get back if you really want my help." Lupe had a twinge of the old days when she and David were always doing things together. If only Papa was driving them to the East Side Field. The idea of doing something for the East Side kids began to appeal to Lupe.

CHAPTER 19

L upe sat frozen in her chair, unwilling to look directly at Mr. Ramirez. She had no excuse for not visiting Mr. Ramirez after his stroke. She couldn't remember if David had gone by after his court hearing to thank the man for his help. But Lupe could not stand to see him in a worse condition than the first time she met him.

"He asks about you and your team almost every day, honey." Mama was officially working full time as Mr. Ramirez's personal caregiver at the Villa. "Why not come by and watch a game on TV with him? That will give you something to talk about."

Lupe decided Mama had a good idea. She figured she could catch the last four innings of the Dodgers game at the Villa with Mr. Ramirez. His face showed such joy when she entered his room. She was sorry she had not come sooner. Mama welcomed her, but Mr. Ramirez only nodded his head vigorously. Then he turned his face toward the TV screen and began an awful grunting sound.

"He's trying to tell you how the team is doing. Here's a chair, honey; I'll get you something to drink," Mama said.

"But I can't . . ." Lupe couldn't believe how badly the stroke had affected his speech.

"Just let him tell you in his own way. I'll be back in a minute." Mama disappeared down the hall, and Mr. Ramirez's wordless grunting continued. He moved his good arm to swat at the TV screen when the players displeased him.

"Yeah, I know. Can you believe it?" Lupe began to respond with neutral comments. She pretended that they were really having a conversation. Mr. Ramirez looked at her and nodded his head in agreement, much to her surprise. Their visit continued with the grunting and agreements for four innings. When the Dodgers squeaked out a victory, both Ramirez and Lupe cheered. They tried and missed each other's hands on a high five. At that moment, Mama reentered the room.

"Time for bed." Lupe recalled hearing Mama say these words a thousand times when she was a child. "This man needs his beauty sleep. Don't you agree?" She was so kind, taking care of Mr. Ramirez as if he were part of the family.

"I need to go anyway; we have a game tomorrow." Mr. Ramirez grunted again, and Lupe assumed he was wishing her luck. "Thanks. My mama will let you know how it turns out."

Ramirez barely raised his right arm and pointed at her. She knew he was saying, "You come back and tell me yourself, Lupe."

As she hurried toward the front doors, Lupe caught a glimpse of a man in the lobby area, reading the Sports section of the newspaper. She knew it was really Roberto's ghost. He must have sensed she was there. "It's about time you came for a visit." He turned and looked right at her. "I'm glad you watched a game with him. Our season is almost over."

The following weekend David drove Lupe to the field to coach the children's team and get college credit. She thought she had figured out how to write a lesson plan. Near the last intersection he clutched the steering wheel, his arms held out straight in front of him as Papa's old Chevy screeched to a stop just inches from a bedraggled man in a wheelchair.

"I should have come the other way. These guys are always out here," David said.

The closer Lupe and David got to the East Side Field, the shabbier the neighborhood looked. The field was less than one hundred yards from a homeless shelter whose residents lounged on the street corners during the day.

"This is much worse than our neighborhood. I didn't notice the last time I was here." Lupe rolled up the car window. The field was just beyond a freeway overpass; underneath the roadway, more men slept on the sidewalk, and there were stained walls and smelly sidewalks that served as their lavatory right next to vendors with open carts selling popcorn and fried foods.

"It smells worse in the summer when it's hot, but the homeless are here year-round. You'll get used to it."

Some of the homeless were in wheelchairs, slumped forward. Lupe couldn't tell if they were asleep or passed out. She looked away, thinking of Mr. Ramirez at the Villa. By comparison, he looked well taken care of.

"Here we are." David pulled the Chevy into a gravel parking lot. In front of the car park, four yellowed baseball diamonds stretched out toward a broad boulevard. Entire families were camped out on blankets around baskets and coolers. The children played chase, and the men tossed a baseball between them while the women tended infants.

"Is there a picnic or something? I thought the kids were going to play today." Lupe scanned the scene in front of her. They looked much like the family gatherings she recalled from her childhood, and she wondered how they would make room for an actual game. "This is a party, not a playing field. Who is in charge here?"

"We are in charge today. Get out of the car, and I will introduce you to a few of the parents. Then we can choose our umpires." David opened the trunk and pulled out extra balls and bats.

"We choose the umpires? You must be kidding." This was nothing like Lupe had in mind when she agreed to coach a kids' team.

"Get over yourself, college girl, and help me carry some of this stuff." David locked the car. For the next half hour Lupe watched her brother take charge, something she had not seen for a long time. His personality transformed into a friendly coach, introducing his kid sister to parents, players, even ice cream vendors, all of them speaking Spanish and enjoying themselves atop the designated baselines and in the outfield. Little by little the families regrouped toward the bleachers and on the outskirts of the diamond.

"Don't worry, you'll get to know everyone very soon, and your Spanish will come back to you, too." David unlocked a wooden supply box at the end of one team bench, and the older kids lined up behind him, taking the bases, the home plate, catcher's gear, and finally the four umpires' chest protectors to their designated spots.

"Mr. Gomez is one of our best umpires." David handed the man his protection. "Especially since his kids are too old to play in this division anymore. This is my kid sister, Lupe. She'll start with the little sluggers in the second game today."

"*Hola, mija.*" The man sounded and looked like he could be an uncle, but Lupe had doubts about his ability to umpire. She looked to her right and left to see that the team benches were already filled with kids squirming and punching each other in the shoulder. There were no uniforms, but the kids on one bench had blue armbands and the others wore orange.

"Okay, it's Dodgers, blue, and Padres, orange, today." David stood between the benches. "Ricky, what are you and Marco both doing on the Dodgers bench? Break up and one of you will need to change your colors." He was pointing to the boys as he called them out. "Same for you, Carlos and Tommy."

"They don't even know what teams they are on?" Lupe watched the confusion and impromptu organizing.

"We try to put together evenly matched groups, depending on who shows up on a given day. The most consistent kids rise to the top. You'll see." David pulled a whistle and a coin from his pocket.

"Okay, let's flip a coin and play ball." One boy approached from each bench, and the play began. David's style of coaching was so natural. Something about his voice reminded her of their Papa. Could she do as good a job? It was Lupe's turn to gather up the younger players who would be her responsibility.

The East Side Field joined four diamonds together. One of the four was used for the little sluggers—in other words, the girls. This was Lupe's assignment. After David got his teams ready for play, Lupe assessed the half-pints skipping around the remaining diamond. Some settled into small groups who sat down on the field and chatted. Others dragged their feet through the dirt and left lines and trails while they picked dandelions off the overgrown field. As always, a few youngsters stood by themselves, isolated from the larger group. Lupe used her newly issued whistle and called the group together around home plate.

"My name is Lupe and I'll be your coach. That's something like a teacher. The first thing we are going to do is take a walk together. Follow me." The young would-be players trailed behind her. Some whispered. Some turned to wave at their parents, who sat on a bench anxious to see their daughters play ball. Lupe stopped at first base and the group gathered around her.

"Do you know where we are?" Lupe asked. A few of the girls called out and the others looked down at their dusty shoes. "That's right, first base! This is like the first line in a story. You begin your run here and finish the story at home plate." Lupe hadn't planned to say this and wondered why it popped into her mind. "Now, what's this?" she held the ball high up and continued as planned. Everyone knew the answer.

"It's a baseball!" they all called out together.

"Now that we know the baseball, let's get to know each other. Say your name, nice and loud, and pass the ball to the next girl." The group began her brand-new training exercise for new young players. *It's about the players and how they work together,* she thought to herself as she heard the girls call out their names and pass the ball.

When everyone had held the ball and said their name, she gave instructions. "Now we are walking again, this time to second base. Follow me, team." This time there was more chatting among the players who now knew at least one other girl's name. "Stop right here and repeat 'second base!'" They shouted it out together.

Some of the parents observing their girls began to get up and walk away from the bleachers, especially the men. But the girls were fully engaged as they walked from base to base, then through the field positions. Each time they made a larger circle and tossed the ball from one girl to another, repeating their names. Some had a hard time tossing and catching the ball, but they got a little better at every position until they all stood at home plate once again.

"We all made it home!" Lupe said. "When we play our games, this is one of the best things."

"What's the best, Coach?" One pigtailed player called out, taking Lupe by surprise.

"I'll show you. Everyone put your hand in the middle, right here." Lupe led the group through their first team cheer, and it seemed the best way to end her first lesson.

CHAPTER 20

"**P**urpose? That's dumb. The purpose is to win the game. That's it." Lupe grumbled as she examined the lesson plan forms on the cafeteria table. Amelia sat next to her.

"Look down here at the notes." Amelia pointed to the small print at the bottom of the paper. "The purpose is your overall goal for one class period," she read. "What did you do with those kids last Saturday?"

"Are you kidding? At first, I could barely get them to listen to me. Finally, I just lined them up and walked the bases with them. It was hopeless." Or was it? Lupe smiled as she recalled the group calling out their names and tossing the ball to one another. She paged through twelve forms in the stack. Each one started with the word *purpose*.

"You know what? I think I get it. My first practice wasn't half bad," Lupe said.

"What is Coach Ferguson always yelling out to us when we miss a catch or drop a ball?" Both girls began to laugh and put their hands on their hips, mocking their coach.

"Team play, girls!" they said together.

"Okay, purpose . . . team play." Lupe penciled in the first line on the lesson plan form. The girls began to joke about other phrases they heard from their own coach at every practice and every game.

"How about fundamentals?" It was a term Coach repeated again and again. Lupe spread out the six required forms for her college credit.

"Good one, Lupe. And ball control." Now Amelia was in the spirit of this assignment.

"Quick recovery." How often had Coach Ferguson shouted this out to the players on the field? "Defense! Offense!" The terms kept coming from Lupe's memory, and she filled them in on the top line of the lesson plan forms.

She had never thought about the process of learning to play, but making plans for her kids' team taught her how much she knew about the game.

"So what's it like, coaching the kids?" Amelia emptied a paper bag from the fast food vendor on campus.

"Chaos, but kind of fun, actually." Lupe reached for a small bag of chips from Amelia's bag, "Can I have these?"

"Take them." Amelia plunged a straw into a juice box. "I never played when I was a little kid."

"Me neither; I just played catch with my brother." Lupe licked salt off her fingers. "You know, it kind of reminds me of that, except now I'm the big sister."

CHAPTER 21

L upe held her lesson plan assignment with a C- scrawled in the top margin by Dr. Phillips. It was not the grade that she was expecting after all her hard work.

"What do you mean *education theory?*"

"There are actually educators, teachers, who write about various ways to teach," Dr. Phillips said. "Your lesson plans are only game plans for your team—practice schedules and things like that."

"Of course they are. That's how kids learn the fundamentals of softball." Lupe was disappointed after working hard to meet the education class requirements.

"Can you think of any other ways kids learn? Education theory claims there are multiple ways to learn," Dr. Phillips said.

"Well, they are crazy. I coach the same way I learned. It's practical," Lupe said.

"Now you see, you are using a hands-on form of practical education. That's a very modern theory of education," Dr. Phillips said.

"I still don't understand what you are saying. And I need way better than a C- on my lesson plans. I intend to transfer to a university at the end of this year." Lupe slumped down in Dr. Phillips's office chair.

"That's exactly why I'm going to assign a tutor to you for the rest of the semester. Do you know Ron Fink?" Dr. Phillips leaned forward across her desk. "He's a great education student. He's going to be a teacher, and I think he can really help you improve your papers."

"Ron Fink? I've never met him. Does he play ball?" Lupe imagined this tutor as a skinny fellow with a crew cut. "Will he understand what I do with the kids?"

"I'm sure you'll get along. I've asked him to observe your East Side team games on Saturday, and then meet you before class in the library." Dr. Phillips was nodding her head in an encouraging way. "Frankly, this is the only way for you to improve your grades."

"There's no other way?" Lupe squirmed in the chair.

"Just try it. He'll be at your game this Saturday; you can meet him then." Dr. Phillips was still nodding her head up and down.

"I only hope this guy already knows something about softball." Lupe tore up her lesson plan for Saturday's game. "So much for this paper I already wrote."

Ron Fink stuck out like a sore thumb among the parents in the bleachers for the game on Saturday. His short-sleeve dress shirt, hard-sole shoes, and pale face contrasted with the tanned parents in their warm-up suits and tennis shoes.

Betty Brewer, one of the moms who always brought snacks (and plenty of fresh gossip) to the games, brought up Ron Fink in a conversation right away.

"I met your boyfriend, Ron, in the bleachers, Lupe. The other moms were wondering if you ever went out with men,"

Betty purred. "Not everyone cares, but I like to know what kind of woman is coaching our little girls."

Betty looked friendly, but her comments could be deadly. Lupe didn't know how to respond. She didn't want anyone to know that Ron was her tutor, but she hated for them to think that he was her boyfriend. It felt awkward when Ron approached her right after the game.

"I guess you figured out who I am." He had a nervous twitch on one side of his face. "Good game with the kids. I really enjoyed it and have a lot of notes."

"Do you?" Lupe was meeting him for the first time and already regretted the arrangement. "Do you know anything about softball, Ron?" Lupe took a step away from him, not wanting to give anyone the wrong impression about their relationship.

"Well, I know a little. My sister played when she was a kid." Ron opened his notebook to show her his comments on the game.

"You wrote all that about one game?" Lupe could not make out his squiggles and diagrams.

"I never really played sports myself, but I'm a great note taker and a pretty good writer." He glanced over at the mothers, who were watching their conversation with great interest.

"Education theory, right? That's what Dr. Phillips said we're supposed to work on." Lupe spoke in a low voice, keeping an eye on the eavesdroppers lingering nearby. "Whatever that is. So you want to meet in the library before class?"

"That's right. Can you bring a draft of your next lesson plan, and we'll go over that?" Ron Fink seemed anxious to get away from the mothers, too.

As Ron began to walk away, Lupe recalled a paper she wrote in her high school days. "Say Ron! Have you ever studied the geometry of baseball? I'll tell you about it sometime."

CHAPTER 22

L upe's second meeting with Ron Fink, in the campus library before her education class, was not what she expected. She couldn't find him in the main reading room or any of the study centers. When she did locate him in a distant alcove of the library, he looked completely different than he had at the game.

"Hey, Ron. I had a hard time finding you. This is a really private room. I didn't even know it was here." Lupe spoke in a hushed library voice, even though they were the only two people in the small space.

"Good for you. That was your first test." Ron wasn't exactly smiling but had a kind of smirk on his face, like he had a trick up his sleeve. He was casually dressed in a sweatshirt and baggy pants, like he was trying to imitate an athlete.

"You're testing me on the library layout? Let's get to work, Mr. Tutor." Lupe tried to sound funny, but something about his words and looks made her suspicious. She plopped her backpack on a small table and dug out her lesson plan draft. "Here's my assignment. Isn't that what we're working on?

"Here. Sit down and let me take a look." Ron pulled out one of the two chairs in the space. When she sat down, he stood behind her and looked over her shoulder at her paper on the table. "I'm going to show you just a few things that will improve your paper."

"Can you back off a little, Ron?" Lupe felt trapped in the private room with Ron leaning over her shoulder.

"Just look at this first line." Instead of backing up Ron crossed his arm over her chest and pointed to the first line of the paper on the table.

"I don't want any funny business here. Just fix the paper." Lupe sounded stronger than she felt.

"What are you talking about?" Ron straightened up and backed away in a hurry. "Read it." Ron's voice sounded a little shaken.

Lupe hoped she had not misunderstood his movements. Maybe he was clueless about girls. She didn't mean to react so strongly. She read, "Lesson Plan, Game 4, Girls' Softball, by Lupe Lopez." Lupe worried that she had actually frightened him.

"See, right there you want to add something like, 'Based on the theory of X by Y, this lesson plan directs student learning.'"

"That's it? So who is X and what is Y?" Lupe pulled out the chair next to her. "Sit down, Ron. It will be easier to talk to you if you are here." He sat.

"Y is any famous educator. X is his or her theory that learners need a lot of small steps forward." Ron scooted his chair as close to Lupe as he could. The outside of his leg pressed against hers. "You teach one step at a time."

"You're kind of close again, Ron," Lupe grumbled. Was he going to give her any breathing room at all? "Okay, I added that line."

"See how easy that was?" Ron leaned over to whisper in Lupe's ear and slid his arm over her shoulders. "We're going to make a lot of progress."

"Hey, weirdo." Lupe pushed her chair back and stood up. "Just because you are smart doesn't mean you can crawl all over me." Lupe was not using her library voice. She was loud and angry.

"Okay, calm down." Ron smiled up at her. "Do you want a better grade, or don't you? We'll meet here, once a week, until the end of the semester. You're going to learn to trust me, even like me."

"How many times have you pulled this routine?" Lupe hoisted her backpack onto her shoulder. "We'll take it one week at a time, and I am done for today, you creep." She stormed out of the library, already late for class.

"Who does he think he is?" Lupe muttered while she suited up for practice and the library scene replayed in her mind.

"What are you grumbling about now?" Amelia dressed at the next locker.

Lupe was too embarrassed to tell Amelia what had happened at her first tutoring session. She didn't want anyone to know that she needed help to pass her education class.

"Cheer up, for goodness' sake." Amelia pulled a plastic bag out of her locker. "Here. Snacks." She held the bag out to Lupe.

"Great! I'm starved," Lupe said. "Thanks."

"It's not for you. I saved it for your tortoise—what do you call her? Shelly?" Amelia repacked her locker and secured it. "I had a gigantic salad for lunch and couldn't finish all of it."

"But you've never even met Shelly." Lupe peeked into the bag. "How nice of you." Amelia was really nice, yet Lupe had never invited her home.

"It's just scraps." Amelia pulled on her sweatshirt. "You've told me so much about Shelly, I kind of feel like I know her."

"Is it weird that I talk about a tortoise as if she were my friend?" Lupe put the plastic bag in her backpack.

"No. All I know is that you seem happy whenever you talk about her." Amelia laughed. "That's the best kind of friend to have."

"Your papers have improved, Lupe." Two weeks later, Dr. Phillips handed back her latest paper with a B in the top margin. "I guess Ron is really helping you out, eh?" Lupe wondered for a moment if Dr. Phillips was in on Ron Fink's scheme to corner girls in his private library study room.

After week three of the library tug-of-war, Ron Fink made a strategic error. He gave Lupe a summary sheet titled, "Five Major Twentieth-Century Education Theorists."

"Wow, I guess you are really a smart guy, Ron. This paper explains everything," Lupe said.

"Yeah, I wrote it for Dr. Phillips last year. That's why I get paid to tutor all the failing students." Ron sounded smug and very proud of himself.

"Why look. There's just enough information for me to use it for the rest of the semester." Lupe waved the paper in his face.

"You still need my help. Dr. Phillips said so."

"No, I think I've got everything I need right here. Plus, I can enlighten Dr. Phillips about your very own twisted education theory." Lupe tucked the paper in her bag. "Go out and find yourself a girl, Ron. You need one bad," Lupe said. "I've got what I need right here—five theorists. Bye."

Later that evening, Lupe sat in the backyard, ready to have her evening chat with Shelly.

"Do you ever get lonely? Maybe I should have bought you a sister, maybe even a mate, but I never thought of you being lonely. Like me." Lupe fed Shelly Amelia's leftover salad scraps.

There was a big full moon hanging directly above the garage, brightening the yard like a spotlight. Lupe noticed the sand patterns in Shelly's box; she watched her tortoise eat before she went back into her house.

"I guess being alone is not so bad, especially on a nice night like this. But sometimes I wish there was someone else for us to talk to."

BOOK REPORT

TITLE: The Modern Theories of Education
CLASS: Education
TEACHER: Dr. Phillips
STUDENT: Lupe Lopez
DATE: January 10, 1995

I am a college-level softball player competing in the California Intercollegiate Federation of Athletics. I am also a children's league coach. My dedication to my sport has grown over six years of practice. My interest in the development of young players directed my academic interests and recently led to this study combining my coaching skills and my understanding of theories of education.

This paper is based on my weekly lesson plans prepared for the local youth softball coaching and competition schedule. When my education class required that I identify the educational theory used to prepare my lesson plans for my team, I had to investigate the options available for my practical teaching assignment.

As a dedicated athlete, I was unaware of any educational theory beyond the rules and regulations of my sport. In the weekly preparation of my lesson plans and the preparation of this paper, I began to recognize several education theorists that are relevant to the game of softball.

The theorists discussed in this paper include the following: John Dewey, Jean Piaget, B. F. Skinner,

Howard Gardner, and Paulo Freire. Of those educators, Dewey's school of Progressivism was the most obvious link to my work with children and physical education due to his focus on the development of critical thinking and problem-solving skills through active engagement. I was especially drawn to his beliefs that students should have a say in their learning processes. The game of softball is a constant application of critical decision-making and active engagement.

A distant second to John Dewey was Jean Piaget and his school of Social Constructivism, which claims learners develop their own understanding and knowledge of the world, and in my case, the game of softball. Some of my lesson plans were designed to avoid rules and regulations and to allow the learners, my players, to be active creators of their own knowledge of how the game works.

B. F. Skinner's behaviorism was the least successful application for my softball lesson plans and student success. His educational theory emphasized the role of reinforcement and punishment in learning. The development of programmed instruction for sports was too strict and inhibiting for my young players. His systems of incentives and rewards worked against the development of team spirit.

Howard Gardner and his theory of multiple intelligences tells us that humans have many types of intelligences, such as language, logical-mathematical, musical, bodily movement, and spatial awareness, as well as interpersonal and intrapersonal intelligence. As a coach I began to watch my players and tried to identify their special skills and how that increased their abilities on our team. This theory suggests that teaching methods should vary to cater to different types of intelligences.

Finally, the work of Paulo Freire in critical pedagogy claims that education is political and that schools often reinforce existing social inequalities. I was surprised to read his theories and took a special interest, given my own cultural background and the minority community status of many of my young players. Freire's theory emphasized the need for education to be empowering, advocating for a relationship between the teacher and student. If I were to go further in the field of education, I would try to learn more about Freire and how this could affect children engaged in sports.

I'm glad I have this extra support and information as I pursue my athletic career and as I lead younger players into an appreciation for and expertise in the game of softball. Previous to this education class, I would have never guessed there was much to learn from educational theorists as it applies to sports. Now I know differently and can include this in my future coaching tasks.

CHAPTER 23

After a long day coaching kids at the East Side Field, Lupe and David got into the car to head home. Lupe kept thinking about one little girl she had noticed running back and forth on the sidelines of the boy's games. The child never stood still but occasionally stopped to pantomime a swing with her imaginary bat or throw a rubber-armed pitch. She told David about the girl. Something about this girl looked familiar to Lupe.

"That's Jake's little sister, Celina." David coached her brother's team. "She's a funny little kid, always imitating her brother's moves. You know, she kind of reminds me of you."

"Did I do that when I was little?" Lupe thought maybe it was herself she was seeing in this girl.

"Her mom goes crazy trying to keep track of her and her brother. That much I've seen." David guzzled a cool bottle of water on their way home. "Mom never worried about you that way."

"She didn't? I'm trying to remember her in those days," Lupe said.

"You were Papa's little girl. He probably tossed as many baseballs to you as he did to me." David looked straight ahead as he drove. His voice had an edge to it.

"And look at us now, surrounded by little sluggers." Lupe tried to bring a smile to her brother's face. "How's her brother as a player?"

"He's okay. I get the feeling he's always looking around for someone. Probably his father," David mumbled.

"Doesn't he come to the games?" Lupe liked the way David thought about his young players.

"He's there at the beginning, but he kind of disappears by the second inning. Who knows what his deal is. But his kids are cute." David raised his eyebrows and shook his head.

Lupe looked away and tried to decide if she should tell David about her experience with Ron Fink, her horny tutor. She knew it would make him mad, so she tried to ease into the story.

"I'm not sure I made the right decision to go to City College. But coaching these kids is fun, even though their parents can be a bit of a pain. Maybe you've got the right idea, spending all your time at the East Side Field."

"It's fun, but it's also a dead end, Lupe. You're smart. I'm a dropout. What's really bothering you?" David moved into the slow lane of traffic. She could see he was in big brother mode. "Tell me."

"It's not just one thing. There's always another roadblock—a teacher who is too tough, a teammate who always seems ready to pick a fight. My books cost more every semester, even though I buy them from the used bookshelves in the student store." Lupe spoke slowly, not wanting to get to the real point. "Then there's the guys."

"What guys?" David blurted out. He was on full alert.

"Well, no one in particular, but there was this stupid tutor in my education class." Lupe hesitated, not sure she should give any details about Ron Fink and his roaming hands.

"You had a tutor? How did you pay for that?" David's thoughts went right to money.

"He was assigned by my teacher. It didn't cost me anything. I think he got class credit for the time he spent with me." Lupe said as little as possible. She realized she had never had a serious conversation about boys with her brother before. Certainly not about dating or sex or anything like that, though she guessed he was probably pretty experienced.

"Did he teach you anything? Was he any good?" David asked.

Lupe's mind replayed the incidents when Ron Fink cornered her in a small room in the library, how he leaned into her and tried to wrap his arms around her.

"Ah, he was okay. Just kind of a creep, you know?" she said.

"What do you mean, a creep?" David's voice was getting louder, even as her description of Ron Fink was getting fainter and more vague. "Did he say something? Did he do something?"

Lupe knew she didn't want to go into any more detail; David was already too worked up and wanting to know everything.

"Nothing I couldn't handle and I did end up with better grades on my education papers." Lupe thought that was an honest account. "Like I said, it's always something coming up just to get through the semester, or to keep peace on the team, or to deal with these Little League parents who think they know better than the coach."

"You got that right. But really, let me know if some guy gives you any trouble, and I'll take care of him." David pulled the car back into the fast lane, and Lupe was glad the conversation was over.

The next Saturday at the East Side Field, Lupe kept an eye out for Celina. She hoped to get the girl engaged with her team of little sluggers. But once the game began, it was all Lupe could do to keep her players in control, looking, throwing, and running in the right direction.

It became a bigger challenge than she could have imagined. Her careful lesson plans prepared for her education class never worked out. Even though the young girls' games were shorter than the boys' games, they took all her energy and attention. After her team finished, Lupe relaxed by watching David's team conclude their game.

Sitting on the sidelines, Lupe spotted Celina with her parents, both of them. She was surprised to see that Celina's mother looked to be about her own age, twenty or so. Her father had on some very tight jeans.

Lupe calculated that the little girl was six and her brother was eight. How young was their mother when she was first pregnant? Twelve or fourteen—no way! Just then, Celina's father caught Lupe watching them and strode right up to her.

"Okay, I've seen you staring at me. I can read your secret thoughts," he said.

"I don't know what you're talking about. I was looking at your cute little girl. I coach the girls' teams," Lupe stammered.

"Sure, go ahead and play hard to get." He smirked. "I know your type."

"I'm Lupe Lopez. My brother, David, coaches your son's team. He's just over there." Lupe pointed to David, glad to have him nearby.

"David Lopez, that jailbird? Are you a bad kid, too? Want to get into some trouble with me?" He laughed. Celina's father hadn't bothered to introduce himself. Lupe couldn't tell if he was joking or just obnoxious.

"You must be joking. Isn't that your wife and kids right there?" Lupe was flabbergasted. Had he really said what she thought he'd said? From the corner of her eye, she could see her brother watching her as he collected his team's gear.

"And, by the way, my brother is not a jailbird." Lupe walked past the obnoxious man and headed straight toward his wife and kids. His daughter, Celina, and her mother were packing up the family's cooler with the snacks they brought to the game. Lupe approached, still blushing from her encounter with this poor woman's rude husband.

"Hello, I'm Lupe Lopez, the coach for the girls' team. I'd love to have your daughter play with the other girls." She bent down to see the girl's mother. The woman, who looked enough like her to be a sister, gave her a confused look.

"*Juega*, mama!" Little Celina was jumping up and down with excitement.

"*Que dice?*" The mother stood, looking back at Lupe. She didn't understand English.

Lupe saw a woman her own age, responsible for two young children, new enough in the States that she spoke no English, with a flirty husband who could do and say whatever he wanted. Now he was explaining things to his wife in Spanish. He called her *Chata,* a not-so-nice nickname that Lupe had heard before.

Lupe tried to piece together her own limited Spanish. "*Señora, su hija es muy bonita. Lleno de energia. Tenemos un equipo especialmente por las ninas. Necesitio su permiso.*" she said, asking permission for her daughter's participation on the team. It was like she was looking at someone in her own family, born in another country, speaking a different language.

"Forget it. I give all the permissions in the family." Celina's father broke into her faltering conversation. He had his thumbs wedged behind his big belt buckle. "My name is Carlos Andrade and we have a deal." Carlos stuck his hand out toward Lupe, daring her to make direct contact with him. His wife and the children giggled. "We will see you, Lupe Lopez, next Saturday and every Saturday after that." He winked as he squeezed her hand.

CHAPTER 24

"I see you met the dashing Mr. Andrade." David always took the same route home after their Saturday games, heading first for a bucket of spicy fried chicken for dinner.

"Chicken again?" Lupe complained. "It makes your breath stink!"

"I like it. Mama likes it, too. And it's cheap." David turned into the drive-through lane. "Who do you need to keep your breath sweet for?"

"Very funny. Yes, I met that very rude man, Carlos. Not that he has anything to do with my breath," Lupe rushed to add. "Celina is going to join my team next week."

"Carlos, eh? Just be sure you don't get two for one." David glanced her way. His dark eyebrows were knit together. "Okay, little sister?"

"What do you mean? She's a cute kid, and I'll be glad to have her join us." Lupe knew David was referring to Celina's flirty father. She'd seen her brother watching her when she spoke with Carlos Andrade at the field. Did he know something more?

"I know guys like that. His old lady takes care of the kids, and he's as free as a bird," David said.

"His old lady?" That phrase always made Lupe mad. "Have you seen his wife? She's barely my age."

"Exactly. And if you haven't noticed, she looks like you, except she's got two little kids hanging all over her." David nodded, proud of his observations. "I'm just saying, you are just his type." The drive-through line was slow. "Stay sharp, little sister." Lupe squirmed to look away from David and looked out the passenger window.

"You're crazy." Lupe tried to change the subject. "Hey, I'm pitching again this week against the Fresno team and in the tournament, too." Lupe hoped the conversation would turn away from Carlos Andrade, whose tight jeans and big belt buckle were etched in her memory.

The SBCC vs. Fresno game was the last regular one before the league's Thanksgiving softball tournament.

Lupe, Amelia, and the rest of the team had high hopes for walking away with a league trophy. Coach Ferguson kept warning them, "Stay sharp and be sharp—no distractions."

"This year is going by so fast. Do you think we're ready?" Amelia tossed the ball to Lupe as they warmed up before the Fresno game.

"I'm ready; let it happen." Lupe wound up and let the ball go. "Between our games and those little kids on Saturday, I feel like a pro."

"How much longer are you going to do that job?" Amelia worked as a part-time waitress at a local café. "Don't those parents drive you crazy?"

"Some of them do." Lupe tried not to think of Carlos Andrade, but he kept creeping into her head. "I like working outside with the kids. I'll do it until I go to university." *What will happen when I move away?* Lupe wondered.

The Fresno game was a great win for the SBCC team. They were on their way to the tournament. It was almost too good to be true. Every once in a while, Lupe glanced at her teammate, Amelia, and hoped their friendship would last forever. She remembered Penny, her best friend from high school, and wondered how her freshman and sophomore years had been. Penny's team was not in the same league as SBCC, so the old friends never met on the field. Lupe could have called her house during the holidays, but something had stopped her. Was she still the team catcher? She must have made new friends right away. Did she have a steady boyfriend? Would Lupe ever stop competing with Penny? Of course she had a boyfriend.

If Amelia was Penny, she could tell her about Carlos Andrade and how he had come on to her. She could have confessed to Penny that she was weirdly drawn to his bad-boy style, but she didn't feel comfortable saying such things to Amelia.

Coach Ferguson had seemed so friendly when Lupe first met her at the summer softball camp. She became increasingly tense as the league championship tournament drew closer. At first, Lupe thought she was the only one drawing extra criticism from the coach. Then she began to hear complaints from other team members. The week before the tournament was especially bad.

"Okay, today we're only going to focus on first base during practice. Everybody who plays in the outfield can go home." Coach Ferguson clutched her clipboard, a whistle hanging around her neck. She wore the same shorts and hoodie, both Nike, as she did every day. Her shoes were the only thing not Nike about her. A big *N* near her heel screamed New Balance.

There was a long story she liked to tell about the importance of sports shoe selection to anyone who had an hour to spare.

"You must be kidding. We're not practicing as a whole team today? What about throwing into first from the field?" the outfielders protested, even though they were just given the afternoon off by their coach. "What about coming in for backup when we have a bunter at the plate? What about calling the foul along the foul line? Why are you splitting up the team?"

"We don't need you today. That's all." The coach waved off the protesting players.

"I need them," Ellen, the first base player said.

"Me, too," Sue, the catcher, complained.

"This is a crazy way to practice," Lupe added.

"I only need five players today." The coach continued toward the door to begin practice with half the team. "We can forget the shortstop, too. Now let's get out there."

"You're nuts. How can you just leave out the shortstop?" Jenny stood up, boldly. She played third base and defended Amelia. Now everyone was on their feet. Coach Ferguson had her hand on the door, ready to take the field.

"Well, maybe you have a point there," Coach said.

"Yeah, team!" Everyone cheered.

"Now that's what I want to hear!" The coach yelled back at them and walked back into the middle of the locker room. "We've got to play like a team when we show up at the tournament. This is not a show with one or two stars." She swiveled around to point at each of the team members. "We need one hundred percent participation from one hundred percent of this team." She stepped onto a bench and looked down on the players. "There's only one team in this room and on the field in every game, every day. We've got to think like that, play like that, act like that, and most important, *be* like that, all the time. Now, let's go!"

CHAPTER 25

The league tournament looked and felt completely different from the team's local games.

"If you think we can waltz in and out of here with a shiny new trophy, think again. Look at some of these players." Coach Ferguson told the cold, hard truth. "These women are big and strong and smart. It's that last part that will kill us. We're not competing with a bunch of little girls. Stay sharp!"

The coach loved to use that word, *sharp*, and she saw how distracted Lupe was. Even one hundred miles away from Santa Barbara, Lupe's mind wandered. Even worse, she was distracted by something that had not yet happened. She didn't want to be attracted to Carlos Andrade, but that man crept into her every thought.

During the tournament, Coach Ferguson kept a close eye on Lupe's pitching. She played five of the seven innings in the first two games, and they won, moving forward in tournament play. During the third game, Lupe gave up hits to several batters. The coached pulled her from the mound in the fifth inning.

"My arm is still good, Coach," Lupe grumbled in the dugout.

"It's not your arm I'm worried about," Coach Ferguson said. "We've got this one. Give someone else a chance to pitch, and get your head together." Lupe didn't want to give someone else a chance to pitch. That was her position, and she wanted to be the star who took the team all the way.

The team finished two runs ahead, without Lupe's help. She wanted to take a trophy home and show it off to her kids during her Saturday game. She wanted to brag to someone else, too.

Game 4 was a narrow loss for the team. Lupe felt it was the coach's fault for pulling her midway through the game, even though she had let several runners get into scoring position by just the third inning. Luckily the other leading league contenders lost a game in the same round when multiple errors allowed a stolen base that eventually turned into a run.

"I don't know what's breaking your concentration, Lupe, but that team's loss was a gift to us," Coach said in front of the entire team. Lupe's face burned with embarrassment and anger. Coach called her out in front of everyone. She never wanted to be pointed out as the weak link again. But it was the coach's favorite word, *sharp*, that jogged the memory of David saying to her, "Stay sharp, little sister."

David had seen what was happening to her after she'd encountered Carlos Andrade at the East Side Field. She could never bear her brother's disappointment if she was the reason her team lost in the tournament.

The last game was a real battle. Their opponents were the smart women that the coach spoke of. Their confidence and discipline was impressive. They hustled on and off the field. Their dugout was like a military barricade, all in order and watchful. Lupe liked it when the opposition heckled and hooted, but these players were stoic and driven; they glared at her on the field.

"Stay sharp, little sister." She kept David's words in her mind and blocked out all other thoughts. It paid off in the seventh inning when her pitches flew past the strongest batters and left the bases empty. The SBCC team gained such an advantage that they were able to finish the game, and the tournament, victorious.

During the team photo, the coach held their new trophy high. She smiled for the camera and held up Amelia's hand, flush with their win. Lupe caught sight of someone she never expected to see.

Was it him? She couldn't quite make him out in the glare of the sun. The team's revelry continued with confetti, and sparkling cider squirted throughout the locker room. It wasn't until they were all headed toward the team bus that a cheering fan brushed her shoulder, a man.

She was surprised to see Roberto Clemente's face looking down at her. He bent down to whisper a few words in her ear, and then disappeared back into the crowd. Coach Ferguson had seen the entire incident.

"You are one of the most popular pitchers we've ever had on our team, Lupe." Coach Ferguson was not saying this like a compliment. "You've got one man waiting for you after practice most afternoons, and today this other fellow, one that I've seen several times at our home games, tracked you all the way to this tournament." She wasn't waiting for a reply but kept moving toward her seat in the bus. "I know they're not all your brothers."

"But Coach, I can't help it," Lupe replied.

"What you can help is the way it is distracting you from our games. You better clean up your act, kid." Coach sat down, and Lupe continued toward the back of the bus with Amelia.

CHAPTER 26

Lupe rode the bus home from the tournament. After their initial excitement over their victory, most of the players dozed off during the three-hour ride back to Santa Barbara. She sat next to Amelia, whose head sagged toward her shoulder. Lupe could not sleep. She watched the passing scenery and wondered if life was as confusing for other people as it was for her. Playing ball and going to college was more than enough to keep her busy and usually happy.

Amelia snored just a little and looked so peaceful and uncomplicated while she napped. Lupe imagined what it would be like to be a waitress instead of working with little kids and their parents. Why did Roberto Clemente show up today of all days? And why was the Coach able to see him? Was he, like David, keeping an eye on her? Couldn't a girl have any privacy? After all, they'd won the tournament; what more could anyone ask? So what if she enjoyed Carlos Andrade's attention? Whose business was that?

"Amelia, are you awake?" Lupe nudged her teammate's shoulder. "I've got something I want to talk about." Maybe this was the time they would become really close friends.

"Yeah, yeah, I hear you. What's up?" Amelia straightened up in her seat and pulled her hair away from her face. "Are you going to tell me what's been bothering you?"

"Do you believe in ghosts?" Lupe told Amelia the story of Mr. Ramirez at Villa Santa Barbara and how he introduced her to his ghost companion, Roberto Clemente.

"You're kidding, right?" Amelia spoke in a whisper so she would not awaken the rest of the team. "And you think you saw Clemente at the tournament?"

"He talked to me just before we got on the bus." Lupe watched Amelia's response. If she could trust her with this story, maybe she could work up the courage to tell her about Carlos Andrade and how she couldn't get him out of her mind.

"Is he here now?" Amelia pulled her hair back into a bun.

"Of course he's not on the bus. He doesn't need to take buses. He just shows up." Lupe paused.

"Okay. So what did he say to you?" Amelia seemed really interested.

"He said, *'Cuidate, muchacha.'*" Lupe had heard this phrase all her life, then realized it would mean nothing to Amelia.

"My grandma used to say that. It means be careful, right?" Amelia took the message more matter-of-factly than Lupe expected. "So what are you supposed to be careful about? Is it that married guy who keeps coming on to you?"

"How do you know about that?" Lupe nearly jumped out of her seat. She looked around to make sure no one else was listening to their conversation. "Who told you?"

"Well, that answers a lot of questions. No wonder you've been so distracted." Amelia had an expression on her face that Lupe couldn't read. "One of my straight friends hangs out at the East Side Field where her younger brother has Saturday games. She said she saw an older guy, one of the dads named Andrade, hitting on you." Lupe didn't know what to say.

"One of your straight friends? What does that mean?" Lupe watched as Amelia rolled her eyes.

"Oh, come on. You didn't know?" Amelia shook her head. "I've never really seen you talk to a guy except your brother. If just one man can get you all worked up, my guess is that you are straight, after all." Amelia stood up and tugged at her shorts. "This is weird, Lupe. Do you want a bottle of water?" She headed toward the cooler at the front of the bus.

Lupe was stunned. She thought back to when she'd first met Amelia at sports camp. They'd been friends. Since then, they'd practiced together, studied together, played together. How could she have been so dense? Was she sending out some kind of signal? Lupe felt like a complete idiot. She turned to look at the rest of the team, sleeping peacefully.

"Water?" Amelia held out a frosty bottle for Lupe. "So is this your first time—I mean, in-fat-u-ated and all that?" She took a long gulp of water and studied Lupe's face. "It happened to me in high school. She played second base on our softball team. I used to love watching her turn a double play. That's why I get so annoyed with Skippy. Man, I was a wreck over her."

"Really? So is it the same for, I mean, on both sides?" Lupe was glad she had the water bottle to hang on to. She didn't want to say the wrong thing. "Why didn't you tell me before?"

"Why did it take you so long to tell me about Clemente and the man at the East Side Field?" Amelia sounded so logical, not embarrassed or anything. "It's been almost two years that we've known each other, Lupe, and we are just now having this conversation."

"I am totally embarrassed. I'm sorry." Lupe wanted to hug her friend, and for the first time she hesitated. "This doesn't change anything."

"It just did, Lupe." Amelia glanced down at Lupe's hands hanging at her side. "Look, I'm the same friend you've always known. You just know me a little better now."

"What happened with the girl who played second base in high school?" Lupe let her tense expression relax. She smiled at Amelia.

"Oh, young love. Her parents moved and she transferred out of the school." Amelia smiled back and gave Lupe a little wink. "I was so smitten—is that the word, smitten? I wrote these long letters but was too afraid to send them to her. Love is weird, even when you are alone in it."

"I'm not even in it yet, and it's already weird." Lupe shrugged her shoulders. "I mean, not really; he's married and everything." Lupe held her hands up like she was writing on a billboard. "Imagine the headline: Junior Coach Shacks Up with Player's Dad." Both girls laughed.

"With Player's Mom. I like that better." Amelia could barely spit out the words she was laughing so hard.

That laughter and horrific headline stayed with Lupe when she returned to the East Side Field the next week and shared her trophy photos with her young players. Carlos Andrade watched the entire game, cheering on his daughter, Celina, for the least little thing she did on the field. Over the course of many Saturday games, Lupe could not help but think that he seemed like two different men: the supportive dad and the hopeless flirt. Somehow it actually made her fonder of him.

Santa Barbara Sporting News

A Roll Call from Our Local Teams

Winter 1995

Local Team Wins College Championship

The Santa Barbara City College women's softball team recently brought home a Southern California League Championship award, which is a first in our community. Congratulations, Lady Gauchos! Coach Ferguson beamed with joy as she introduced her team to the SBCC board of trustees and local journalists.

"This is a first-time championship for any of our Santa Barbara teams. Our victory over experienced players in Los Angeles, Orange, and San Diego counties was a surprise to many observers in the college sports world, but it was a natural consequence of the great pool of players SBCC has been able to recruit and support." Coach Ferguson said.

The winning team includes ten players who will take advantage of the existing transfer agreement between the University of California system and the CA Community College District for students graduating with their Associate of Arts degree after two or more years of study.

"Needless to say, we have some recruiting to do since many of our graduating students will be on the roster of UC campuses next season. They will take their athletic and academic skills with them to their new teams."

CHAPTER 27

"**D**on't you find it odd that he watches his daughter's games, while his wife is the one who enthusiastically encourages her son?" David never said anything good about Carlos.

"What kind of sexist thing is that to say? A father supports his daughter's team, and that's wrong?" Lupe found herself defending Carlos the more David put him down. "He even brings treats for the team."

"Treats that his poor wife makes, no doubt," David shot back.

"He gives rides to the other kids," Lupe said.

"And always invites you to go along, right?" David said.

"You would criticize him if he didn't have another adult in the car," Lupe replied.

"Now you are qualified as an adult?" David said.

"Hey, I am an adult to everyone but you. I'll be twenty-one on my next birthday for your information. And I am a coach, in the same way as you are. Perhaps that's what's troubling you?" Lupe hadn't fully processed this yet, but she contemplated the potential truth behind it.

"What's concerning me is that he is getting closer to you, and you are unaware of it. Soon he'll be on our doorstep," David muttered. "Do you realize his wife is going home to

Mexico for Christmas and taking their son with her? The kid told me he'd miss practice for a month."

"She's leaving town? No, I wasn't aware of it." Lupe said.

The next Saturday Celina arrived at softball practice carrying a package wrapped with tissue paper and a ribbon. She skipped ahead of her father, proud to present a gift to her coach.

"For you," she said.

"It's only cookies. My wife thought your mama would enjoy them over Christmas," Carlos said.

"Thank you, how nice. Is it true your mother is going on a trip over Christmas?" Lupe asked Celina.

"My wife's father is sick in Matamoros," Carlos said in a low voice. "She may be gone for some time."

"And she's taking Jake with her?" Now she understood the situation. "He'll miss a lot of school and practice." Lupe was trying not to sound like a nag.

"She thought our son would cheer up the old man. Someday the boy will inherit the family business." Carlos patted Celina's head. "While they are gone, perhaps we can do something together over the holiday." Carlos stooped down to his daughter's level. "We all love Coach Lupe, don't we, Celina?" The girl wrapped both arms around Lupe's leg and buried her head in her hip. Carlos patted his daughter on the head as he moved too close to Lupe and stared straight into her eyes. "You resemble her so much."

"Time to play ball, kids." Lupe pulled away and rounded up her team. She handed the package of cookies back to Carlos. "Here, why don't you take these to my mama yourself? I'll give you the address."

"Twelve thirty Olive Street, right?" Carlos responded.

"How did you know?" Lupe glanced around to check if their conversation was being observed.

"I know a lot about you. I'd love to meet your mama," Carlos said.

Lupe blew the whistle three more times, and the players got settled into their positions. The team was learning to work together. It was particularly thrilling when a player caught a ball and truly understood what to do, tagging a runner and throwing to a teammate. But the biggest thrill by far was hearing the girls cheer for one another. A group of little girls had become a team.

A lot of rumors circulated about a holiday party for the team, so Lupe wasn't taken aback to see a group of mothers waiting to talk with her at the end of the game.

"We need a minute of your time, Coach Lupe." Betty Brewer was the organizer among the mothers. "This won't take long."

"Sure. Great win today. I'm so proud of all your girls and hope you are, too." Lupe's excitement was genuine. When the girls performed well, she had extra patience for the parents who always wanted to give her advice about the game. But, Betty's face looked very stern. Lupe could not imagine what she would complain about this time. "What is it, ladies? Do you think we can improve the game?" Lupe didn't genuinely want their advice, but she knew a major part of coaching kids was keeping the parents happy.

"We've seen you spending time with Celina's dad, Carlos Andrade. It doesn't seem right." The other mothers looked down at the ground and shifted their feet in the dirt. "We assumed it was our imagination, but people are starting to talk. He is a married man with two children, you know."

"I'm fully aware of that, and that's why there is nothing wrong happening at all." Lupe's heart began to pound rapidly. How dare these women accuse her of something? "I don't appreciate any of you feeding this type of gossip."

"Where there's smoke there's fire, young lady. It's obvious how much attention he's been giving you, and it's just not right to have our daughters involved in anything like that." Now the group was gaining courage and glaring at Lupe as they spoke. She felt like she had been caught doing something very wrong. It was true, Carlos gave her a lot of attention, and it was also true that she enjoyed his company and his compliments.

"I can't help what Carlos does. He's a grown man." In fact, Lupe wished he would do more. Was he just teasing her, or would he ever make a definite move? "You have nothing to worry about for your daughters."

"We agree we won't have anything to worry about when we take our girls off your team." Now the women were speaking more loudly, even pointing their fingers at Lupe. "You are walking on thin ice, and you better get your life together."

Three of the enraged mothers and their daughters were gone before Lupe even realized what was happening to her precious team. There were only seven players left. How would she find a way to build up the team? And what about building up her reputation? Then she realized that Carlos was on the way to her house to meet Mama.

As soon as Lupe entered the house, she heard David's complaints.

"He's coming? Mama, we don't want him here." David stomped around the family's pint-size Christmas tree.

"What are you getting so excited about? He just wants to bring a tiny gift." Mama set candles around the Blessed

Mother's statue on the dinner table. It was an old porcelain decoration, bought by Lupe's father. Every Christmas since his death three years ago, the statue was set in a place of honor. "I hope he gets here before five. I have to go to the Villa for Mr. Ramirez's dinnertime," Mama said.

"Can't you be late, Mama?" After all her daydreams, Lupe was nervous about having Carlos Andrade in their home. Why had he known the address before she told him? Her nerves and excitement battled in her chest.

"I can't believe you two are making such a big deal over one stupid plate of cookies." David unlatched the front door. "I'm going outside to put some Christmas lights in the trees." He was only gone twenty minutes when the doorbell rang.

"Merry Christmas, Coach Lupe and Coach Lupe's mama," Celina's squeaky voice called out. She held the wrapped gift, by now, somewhat worse for wear.

"Hay, que chula—what a little doll," Mama cried out. Lupe had not seen so much emotion from her in years.

"Mama, this is Celina. She plays on our team. Celina, this is my mama." Lupe noticed that Carlos did not enter the door after his daughter. Mama scooped up the little girl with a big hug, careful not to crush the cookies.

"Welcome, Celina. You look just like another little girl I once knew." Mama's eyes were all dewy. The next thing Lupe knew, her mother had the little girl on her lap and held the phone in one hand. "Gloria, can you help Mr. Ramirez with his dinner tonight? We had unexpected guests drop in." Mama canceled her work schedule. "This is what we've been missing in this house. She looks just like you used to look, honey."

"Excuse me, I seem to have lost my little girl." Carlos Andrade walked through the front door with David right behind him.

"The lights are up. I had help," David said. "Can I get you a beer, Carlos?" Lupe could not believe her ears. "You know, Carlos gave one bulb a lick and a twist and the whole string lit up." After all his warnings about Carlos, David was treating him like a long-lost cousin.

"You must be Carlos Andrade, how sweet of you to bring a gift and this dear little girl to visit us." Mama was at her charming best.

"I am Carlos, and I feel like I already know you after all Lupe has told me about the family." Lupe had never discussed the family with Carlos.

"And Señora Andrade, the girl's mama? Dónde está?" Mama was not shy.

"She is in Mexico with her own papa, Señor Fuentes, and our son. Thank you for making us welcome here." Carlos reached out for the beer David had brought from the kitchen. With his other hand, he produced a cigarette case and offered it to Mama, then to David.

"None for me. Why don't you boys go out on the porch? That's where my dear husband used to smoke, God rest his soul. We girls will stay in here and visit." Mama sounded like some kind of Southern belle, not a Mexican immigrant. Lupe observed as Carlos captivated both Mama and David right in front of her.

After his beer, Carlos came inside and suggested that Lupe might like to take Celina out to see the stars.

"It's beautiful tonight; go on out." He winked at Lupe as if he was planning a secret.

Lupe took Celina out the back door. It was actually a cloudy night. She stood near the door so she could overhear what Carlos said to Mama.

"It will be such a surprise; she's always wanted a canopy," Lupe heard Carlos saying. "If you can watch her for an hour or so, it would be a great help." Was he asking Mama to babysit?

"Lupe always wanted one. This sounds lovely." Mama's voice was loud enough to hear, but Lupe could not figure out what she and Carlos were talking about.

"You've got a sandbox! Let's play." Celina was ready to climb into Shelly's sandbox before Lupe caught her by the arm.

"It's not that kind of sandbox. My tortoise lives in here. We don't want to step on her." Lupe tried to stay calm but had a horrible image of Celina stomping on Shelly.

"What's a tor-tus? Is it like a kitty that lives in a sand-box?" Celina drew back when Lupe tugged on her arm.

"It's like a turtle. I'm sorry I pulled your arm so hard," Lupe apologized.

"Like the little turtles in the duck pond at the park?" Celina asked.

"Well, this one is not so little. She's old," Lupe said.

"It's a girl turtle? I can't see her." Celina leaned over the edge of the sandbox and dragged her finger in the sand.

"Time to go!" Carlos called out of the back door.

"Look, Daddy. A turtle, a big girl one," Celina said.

"What are you doing?" Carlos raised his voice. "Get your hand out of there—it's dirty."

"She's fine," Lupe said. "She's meeting Shelly."

"Are you crazy? That's dangerous," Carlos yelled and jumped from the back porch to reach for Celina.

"Is everything okay out there?" Mama looked out from the kitchen. The moment she called out, Carlos got his temper under control.

"We're fine, just saying our goodbyes." Carlos covered up his outburst. He picked up Celina, tickling her under the arm.

"Thank Mama Lopez for letting us visit. Maybe we can come back soon."

"It's almost too quiet without that little one," Mama said after Carlos and Celina left. "We arranged it, Lupe. Tomorrow night you'll help Carlos put together a canopy he bought for Celina's bed, and she will stay here with me. I can't wait." Mama held her hands together as if a wish had come true.

"He didn't ask me to help." Lupe's heart went back to beating rapidly. She imagined herself alone with Carlos in his house tomorrow night. The thought provoked both fear and joy.

"It's a surprise, for Celina," Mama whispered. "Just imagine." She had a dreamy look in her eyes as she placed Celina's gift near the Christmas tree.

"No, Mama. Don't imagine anything; I know what you are thinking. Please don't imagine," Lupe said.

CHAPTER 28

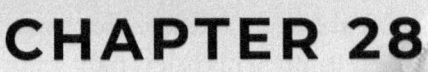

Just before six the next evening, Carlos's car pulled up in the Lopez driveway.

"Ho, ho, ho, Santa is coming soon," Carlos called out as he knocked on the door.

"Hello and welcome back," Mama greeted him cheerfully. "You are just in time for a cafecito!" Lupe overheard everything from her room, which was strewn with outfits she had tried on and rejected for what was supposed to be a casual, project-related night, putting together a store-bought canopy over Celina's bed.

"Fuentes Coffee!" Celina sang out unexpectedly.

"Is that your favorite coffee, Celina?" Mama was amused by her response.

"Her abuelo, Grandpa Fuentes, owns a large coffee plantation in Mexico. It's really a farm," Carlos explained. "That's why I run our little Fuentes Coffee Bar here in town."

"You never told me that." Lupe stepped into the room in her favorite jeans and a silky blouse.

"Well, look at you, pretty blouse, lady." Carlos gave her a thumbs-up, the sign of excellence. It seemed to Lupe that he was in a very good mood.

"We have some special cartoons to watch. Are you ready?" Mama was in a good mood, too. She guided Celina over to the television and waved off Carlos and Lupe behind her back.

Carlos took Lupe's hand and led her outside. Her hands were cold, and she could feel the warmth in his palms right away.

"You didn't really ask me to do this canopy assembly job, you know." She was delighted to leave the house with him, alone, in his car, heading for his home, but didn't want to show how eager she was.

"I asked your mama's permission. Isn't that all we need?" Carlos had a mischievous tone in his voice. On the way to his home, he drove past Fuentes Coffee Bar. "See? There it is; now you always know where to find me."

Lupe had seen the coffee shop many times, but never considered it to be connected to Carlos Andrade. He had been right there all along, but they had to meet at the East Side Field.

"I joke about it, but it's the first business I've ever owned. I even went to business school. It practically wrecked our marriage." Carlos' jovial voice turned more serious than Lupe had ever heard him speak before.

"Really? Was it that hard?" It was the only question Lupe could think to ask, even though she didn't really want to know anything about his marriage.

"It's hard when one person is getting an education and the other has none, or when one person can't really converse about business or even talk to employees." Now Carlos's voice was nearly solemn. "But hey, she and her father are Fuentes Coffee, and I'm just an owner manager."

"Just? You have your own business. I think that's great." Lupe wanted to compliment him. She actually preferred the bold flirt in him to this humble son-in-law tone.

"Thank you, Lupe. Now we get to try our hand at the princess canopy do-it-yourself kit. Ready?" Carlos pulled into a driveway beside a small wood cottage. All the lights were out, and it didn't look at all welcoming.

"It's so dark." Lupe tugged on the collar of her blouse nervously.

"Fear not, I'll protect you." Carlos made a show of opening her car door and escorting her up to the side door. A huge cardboard box was propped up just inside the door. Princess Canopy was printed on the side. "Our work awaits us." Carlos walked ahead of her, flipping on lights as he entered.

Now that they were alone in his house, Lupe was thankful that they had an actual task to accomplish. She read the directions out loud, and Carlos fit the canopy parts together one piece at a time. When all the screws had been tightened and the arched poles rose above Celina's little bed, Carlos paused and took a long look at her.

"Mission accomplished. Thank you, Ms. Lopez," he pronounced formally. "Now, make yourself comfortable. I've got a few things to do. You can relax in the living room, where the grown-ups play."

"Ah, okay." Lupe was not sure what was coming next, but she moved into the living room. Family photos captured her attention right away. Baby pictures of Celina and her brother, Jake, were prominent. A picture of an old man standing in front of a warehouse with a big sign that read FUENTES COFFEE MX sat atop a shelf. In the back corner of that same shelf was a dusty frame with a wedding picture of Carlos and his very young wife, also taken in Mexico. Lupe felt the young bride in the photo was looking back at her and speaking to her; please think of me and my children, she seemed to say. Lupe jumped when she heard Carlos's voice.

"I see you've discovered our history, Lupe. Trust me, it's not what lies ahead." Carlos approached her and gently grasped her hand. "You are the future."

"But this is your family; doesn't that mean anything to you?" He did not respond but instead led her through a short hallway, then opened the door to a bedroom where several candles burned on the dresser.

"Are we setting up another canopy?" Lupe knew it was a stupid thing to say, but she didn't know what else she was supposed to do. "What do you mean 'I'm the future'?" She could not shake the image of his wedding picture from her mind. What was she doing here, alone with this man? Why had she been so full of romantic fantasy?

"You have no idea how much I need you, Lupe Lopez. It's been tearing me apart to be the good dad all these weeks while I'm falling more and more in love with you." He spoke like some rom-com actor and pulled her closer to the bed. "Let's only stay here for a little bit."

"This doesn't feel right, Carlos." Lupe pulled back against his hand, but it was a half-hearted effort. "This is your wife's bedroom."

"Come here, please." He closed the space between them, and they stood face-to-face. His warm breath, with a hint of coffee, brushed her lips. "Celina and I play a game—What If?, we call it. We imagine all the things we want." He sat her on the bed. "Night after night, I've laid here and wondered, What If? You are my 'What If.'"

"Seriously, Carlos?" Lupe refused to sit down. "What if your wife was here? He pressed his lips on the backs of her hands. Did he even listen to what she was saying? Now what? Lupe asked herself. You agreed to come here with Carlos. Now what's going to happen?

A blaring phone rang from somewhere in the house and sent nervous electricity through Lupe's body. She watched Carlos rush toward the ringing phone, and then she moved close enough to hear him speaking rapid Spanish with someone on the other end of the phone. He paced back and forth, completely unaware that she was eavesdropping on the conversation. It was someone he kept calling mi amor, "Si, si mi vida, *cálmate*."

CHAPTER 29

"Mama, I need your help." Lupe entered the house after softball practice on the Monday following the holiday weekend. She gathered all her courage to talk with her mother. She threw her backpack and her softball gear in the corner of the kitchen. She knew she could not be completely honest about why the mothers had pulled their daughters from her team last Saturday. She'd sworn to herself to tell no one about her night with Carlos.

"I hoped you would talk to me about your romance." Mama put a teakettle on the stove. "Can't you put those shoes out on the porch?"

"This is not about romance, Mama. It's about my team, the little girls." Lupe shivered to think of talking to her mama about her so-called love life.

"That's little Celina's team. What can I do to help?" Mama put two mugs on the table.

"I need more players for our last game. I only have seven girls, and I need to put nine on the field," Lupe said. She did not want to explain why.

"What happened to those two girls?" Mama must have sensed that Lupe was holding back crucial information. "There are lots of little girls at the East Side Field with their parents and brothers each Saturday. It should be easy to find two more girls to play."

Just as the tea was poured, David entered the kitchen from the garage. As long as Lupe could remember, her mother-daughter conversations had always been interrupted by her older brother.

"I can't just go up to every parent and ask that their daughter play for our team." Lupe imagined the families who picnicked at the East Side Field each Saturday.

"Isn't that how you got Celina on your team and met her papa, Carlos?" Mom was right about that, but Lupe did not want to think about Carlos and his daughter right now.

"You sure can't. Adding new players at the very end of the season isn't allowed. You have to get permission from the commissioner." David inserted himself into the conversation. "I know her—Bonnie Crane. Maybe I could help you if you made it worth my while."

"David Lopez, you will help your sister because it's the right thing to do. Don't be such a smarty-pants." David and Lupe both laughed at Mama's words.

"Who, me?" David got his own mug for tea. "You need some kind of angle. You could say you are recruiting new players for next season and want to give them a sense of the game." He poured his tea and asked, "Say, why did you lose players so late in the season?"

"Talk to the commissioner? That's actually not a half-bad idea." Lupe hoped he would not notice how she avoided his question. The phone rang and no one made a move to answer it. "I doubt that it's for me. You get it," Lupe said.

"Lopez Softball Recruiters," David joked as he answered the phone.

"This is the manager for the Los Angeles Dodgers," the voice on the other end of the phone line said. Then Amelia burst into laughter. "Hey, David. Is Lupe there?"

"It's Amelia, for you." David handed the phone to Lupe.

"Hi, I'm surprised to hear from you," Lupe said.

"I have a question. Is it all right if I come to your next Saturday game?" Amelia let the question linger with no explanation for her interest. "You know, just to watch?"

"What is it? Something wrong?" David asked.

"She wants to come to the game on Saturday," Lupe said. "Sure, why not? I'm surprised you want to give up a Saturday afternoon. Aren't you working?"

"Tell her to come and wear her uniform," David said.

"What? Why?" Lupe handed the phone back to David. "You do it."

"I heard that. Why should I wear my uniform?" Amelia said over the phone.

"We're sitting here trying to figure out how to fill two spots on Lupe's team this Saturday. If you show up in your uniform and create some interest, I can tell the commissioner we're trying to recruit players for next season." David spoke quickly, waving his free hand. Lupe and Mama listened, trying to follow his plan.

"I don't get it. How does my uniform matter?" Amelia asked.

"To those little kids, you are a big star college player. I'll take pictures, and the kids who pose with you will get to join the game for an inning or two," David explained. "You'll be a draw, get it?"

"Whatever. I just wanted to watch." Amelia spoke slowly. "Let me talk to your sister."

"Actually, it will help me." Lupe stood next to David and spoke into the phone. "Will you do it?"

"Yeah, sure. You guys are nuts. Why do you need to fill spots on your team? Aren't you at the end of your season?" Amelia was as curious as the others, but Lupe kept the answer to herself.

"Great. Thanks." Lupe hung up the phone. "Where are we going to get a camera?" She turned to her brother.

"Go check the box in the garage near the door. Your papa's old camera may be there." Mama sent David out of the kitchen.

"I want to talk, too, Lupe." Mama stood up and closed the door when David headed out to the garage. "I saw how Carlos looked at you, and I know you are more than just friends. It reminded me of how I felt when I met your father."

"Why are you saying this now, Mama?" Lupe did not want to hear what her mama had to say.

"Just listen. I've never told you, but your papa was engaged when I met him. He had promised to marry a girl he'd left behind in Mexico." Mama clutched her tea mug with both hands.

"Well, you got married anyway." Lupe squirmed in her chair as she listened. "Why are you telling me this?"

"He was a proud fellow, rather brash, too. As a matter of fact, your brother reminds me of how your papa used to be. But I couldn't get him out of my mind." Mama hung her head and shook it slightly. "I was very attracted to your papa from the start, but I didn't want to be. I knew he was engaged to that girl. I didn't want to cause any trouble, but . . ."

"But you kept thinking about him? I know how that is," Lupe said.

"It was after your papa and the girl lost contact that we got married. Funny thing: that friend of Mr. Ramirez's— Roberto—knew the whole story," Mama said.

"How could he? He wasn't here," Lupe said.

"He even knew I would take care of Mr. Ramirez when he got real sick. And he knows about you and Carlos, too." Mama lifted her head and looked straight at Lupe.

"Why are you telling me this?" Lupe's head reeled with the news of her father's past. "I don't want to hear it." She could not overcome her shame about her evening with Carlos. Her heart beat fast.

"I am just your old mama, but I know how complicated life can be when you are young." Mama rinsed her cup. "That's all I'll say unless you want to talk about it."

"No, Mama. I don't want to talk about it." Lupe could feel she was blushing. How did Mama know the real reason she needed to talk? Even the mothers at the baseball field knew.

"Does Roberto Clemente know everything?" Lupe held her breath. Was she being watched?

"He told me not to worry." Mama patted her shoulder.

CHAPTER 30

At two o'clock on Saturday afternoon, it was time for Lupe's last regular season game at the East Side Field with her young players.

"Have you seen Amelia? Did you remember to bring Papa's old camera?" Lupe's stomach was in a knot.

"Would you calm down?" David looked over his shoulder toward the commissioner and waved. "She thought this was a great idea. She's always trying to get more kids to sign up for teams."

"Are you sure she will allow the new kids to fill in for this one game?" Lupe worried about David's scheme.

"Take it easy. I told you it would work." David helped drag Lupe's team gear to the dugout. "Look, there's Amelia coming across the field in her uniform. She looks like the Pied Piper of softball." A trail of young girls ran alongside Amelia and reached out to give her high fives.

"Get ready with the camera." Lupe tried to corral the kids onto the bench for a photo and a pep talk. "Sit here, Amelia. We're ready." Amelia was having a ball, pretending to be some kind of superstar.

While David snapped photos, Lupe couldn't help but scan the bleachers behind the bench. She was anxious to see

Carlos arrive with Celina. She was worried about the team mothers hearing more gossip, now the truth, about her and Carlos.

"Which of you girls want to play with our team today?" Lupe tried her best to sound enthusiastic and inviting. The little girls' hands shot up in the air.

"I do! I do!" At least Lupe could stop worrying about not having enough players to finish her game.

"Amelia, would you lead our new players into the out-field and show them where to stand?" With such a young team, Lupe knew few, if any, hits would make it as far as the outfield.

"You got it, Coach. Come on, team." Amelia led her fans onto the field.

It was then that Lupe spotted Carlos and Celina approaching. Carlos barely raised his hand to give her a wave and looked away as soon as their eyes met. He bent down to talk to Celina, then gave her a little pat on the behind to send her over toward Lupe.

"Go team!" The opposition's bench was starting to fill up, including the two girls who played with Lupe until their mothers removed them at the last minute. There was a lot of enthusiasm from the other side. Lupe spotted Betty Brewer and her gossipy friend scowling at her and whispering with their hands held up to cover their mouths. Betty Brewer even had the nerve to point to Carlos in the opposite bleachers.

"Okay, let's play ball, ladies," the umpire called out to start the game.

Focus, Lupe told herself. She saw Amelia leave the new players in the field and head for the bleachers. To her surprise, Amelia seated herself right next to Carlos. Lupe couldn't allow herself to think about that. She focused on her regular players in the infield.

The game proceeded at such a slow pace that Lupe had plenty of time to observe Betty Brewer giving the other coach a hard time about giving her daughter time to play. Lupe also kept an eye on her team's new recruits in the outfield. She couldn't blame them for losing interest when the ball didn't even come close to them.

Lupe's new second base player, Audrey, was the cheerleader for the entire team. She kept the chatter up among the players, heckling the opposing team. She led the cheers at the end of an inning when the opposition was shut out.

What was Amelia talking to Carlos about in the bleachers? That was foremost on Lupe's mind. Was this why she was so anxious to come to the field, even willing to dress in her SBCC uniform and pose for photos with the little girls?

In the last inning of a scoreless game, Betty Brewer finally got her way when the opposing coach relented to her demands and put her daughter on the field at second base. Lupe's team was working its way through their batting order. The pitching was so bad, the players rarely got to take a real swing at the ball.

Then Audrey, Lupe's second base player, came to bat. By now she was a crowd favorite because of all the enthusiasm she had shown in an otherwise dull game. There was so much chatter and cheering on the field that a passerby might have thought the scoreless game was an exciting slugfest. An overanxious Audrey missed the first two pitches but connected on the third.

It was a hot one-hopper that went past the pitcher and headed toward second base. Betty Brewer's daughter was caught off guard. Her reaction was too slow, and the ball ricocheted off her mitt and dribbled out toward center field. Instead of chasing the ball down, she collapsed on the field in frustration and embarrassment. Her mother screamed and put up a fuss. The center fielder finally realized she needed to pick up the ball that was rolling in her direction.

Audrey kept running past second base. The crowd roared for her. There was no coach posted at third base. Audrey glanced toward Lupe to get a go-ahead sign, and when Lupe waved her on she kept running and jumped triumphantly on home plate. That one run in the last inning was the grand finale of the game, made all the more satisfying by the uncontrolled frustration suffered by Betty Brewer.

With the winning run on the scoreboard, Lupe allowed herself to look toward where Amelia sat next to Carlos. Neither one was in the bleachers. Lupe spotted them far beyond the team bench talking with great animation, hands flying in the air, their faces red and strained.

The team crowded around Lupe, their parents joining the celebration and cheers. The regular players were high-fiving the new recruits. Parents held cameras high and clicked memorial photos. Even the commissioner herself approached the victors to give her congratulations and provide sign-up forms to the new players.

Lupe was so torn between her team and wanting to locate Carlos and Amelia, she could hardly keep track of all that was going on until she saw a red-faced Betty Brewer approaching the commissioner. Would she make her accusations public?

"Let's get a team shot with the commissioner." David approached with Papa's old camera in hand. "Team members only," he said, separating the commissioner from all the adults and placing her at a safe distance from Betty Brewer. Lupe didn't know whether David was aware of the accusations that Betty spread or whether holding the camera and ordering people around was motivating him. Betty's daughter, humiliated by her own error and her pushy parent, pulled her mother away.

"Now the parents and the commissioner, and now, the players with Coach Lupe," David instructed the crowd. He sounded so professional the entire group followed his directions.

Still, there was no sign of Carlos or Amelia. Even Celina had left the field without Lupe noticing. It was a troubling realization for Lupe, one that she would not understand until much later.

Santa Barbara Sporting News

A Roll Call from Our Local Teams

Spring 1996

Youth League Season Concludes

City Youth League Commissioner Bonnie Crane congratulated young players at East Side Field last Saturday for their winning performance on the girls' softball team coached by SBCC pitcher, Lupe Lopez. The rookie players aged seven to nine years, learned sport fundamentals and team play in this family-oriented environment.

This multigenerational gathering hosts parents and grandparents as spectators and brothers and sisters as new players at our historic East Side Field. Some coaches, like Lopez, are also able to garner educational credits for their work with the young players.

Commissioner Bonnie Crane reminds parents to enroll their children in next year's youth league by calling her office at (555) 574-3030.

CHAPTER 31

L upe was ready to graduate and transfer to the university with a softball scholarship. The end of her sophomore year as a City College student athlete was just weeks away. She knew she had to keep her focus. Two years ago, her high school team deteriorated in the last few games, and her scholarship turned to dust. She would not let that happen again.

She was poised for a pitch with the batter in her sights. The team was experienced, road-tested, and the exact opposite of the little girls who played at the East Side Field. The batter made a show of banging her bat on her cleats. Lupe could not let her thoughts slide to her future. *Wake up!* Lupe thought as she pulled herself back into the action of the game.

The team led by a fragile margin, 7–5. This batter could shatter that lead in one swing if Lupe threw a fastball. The runner at first was ready to steal second.

Lupe packed her resolve into the power of her pitch. The batter, not expecting the curveball, swung violently at the oncoming ball loaded with her future dreams. Even before the bat and ball connected, the runner at first dug into her stride toward second. The ball moved low and slow through the right side of the infield, behind the runner who tagged second and kept going until the coach at third told her to stop.

Of course, Skippy was out of position and let the ball roll into right field. The fielder scooped it up but threw beyond home plate into the backstop. The catcher moved to get the ball, and Lupe darted forward to cover home.

The runner saw the error and decided to go past third and beat the ball home. She barreled toward Lupe, who positioned herself, straddling the plate; her right leg extended and dug in.

"No way are you getting past me." Lupe couldn't tell if she said it out loud, but the words strengthened her entire stance and resolve. *We can handle this,* she thought. Without looking, she knew that the catcher had finally run down the ball and would deliver it to her.

One moment she was concentrating on tagging out the runner, the next she heard the sound of her shin bone giving way. When she and the runner collided, the crowd gasped. The pain was blinding, but Lupe clutched the ball and let her head fall back into the dirt. She only wanted to hear the call. Finally it came when the umpire cried, "You're out!"

When Lupe dared to open her eyes, she could see Coach Ferguson and the team doctor hunched over her. She heard the wail of an approaching siren and the faint sound of Amelia repeating her name.

"Lupe! Lupe! Lupe!" It reminded her of the cheer her young players gave her when they won their game at the East Side Field the week before.

Santa Barbara Sporting News

A Roll Call from Our Local Teams

Spring 1996

City College Player Injured Saving Game

Santa Barbara City College softball pitcher, Lupe Lopez, landed on the injured list while protecting home plate for a team win in the seventh inning on April 12. She is expected to miss the remainder of the season. The scrappy player is known for her dedication to her team and her performance. Sports medicine specialist Aaron Kaplan made an announcement after treating the injury. He recommended total immobilization, using a cast on the shin to promote healing.

"Slow and steady wins the race or, in this case, the ball game," Kaplan said.

The attending physician emphasized the stress that a sports injury can cause an athlete. While Lopez will not be able to participate in softball games with an immobilized leg, the physician may give her crutches, or a wheelchair, so she can attend games and cheer on her team. "The advanced techniques and medical equipment will help to heal this softball injury, but only the family, her friends, and her team will ease the mind of this outstanding athlete."

CHAPTER 32

L upe spent three days after her injury at home in bed with her leg propped up. Mama and David took turns taking care of her, bringing in food, setting up a TV she could watch, and keeping her company. Mama was in charge of her prescribed pain medications.

"Is it time? My leg is throbbing." Lupe just wanted to be numb and sleep.

"We're supposed to cut back on these pills after three days," Mama said.

"How long have I been here? I'm losing track of time in this bed," Lupe said.

"The game was Thursday, this is already Sunday." Mom counted up the days.

"Just one, Mama, and then I can sleep." Lupe knew she was pushing the limits of her pain pills. "On Monday we can stop."

"I've got to get to work. David will be here with your dinner later." Mom reached in her purse for the prescription medications. "This will be your last one." She held up a capsule to Lupe's lips and handed her a glass of water.

Settled back in her pillows, Lupe heard the front door close after Mama left for work. The house was peaceful, so quiet she could hear her own heartbeat. She counted the beats and soon fell into a deep sleep.

Her mind kept replaying the moment of her collision at home plate, the crowd of emergency workers surrounding her, the coach looking so anxious, and Amelia calling her name.

"It wasn't your fault. You did the right thing running in to cover home."

Someone, a man, had entered her room and spoke in a sympathetic voice. Was it Carlos, coming to see how she was? Lupe struggled to open her eyes but realized they were still shut tight.

"That out saved the game for your team, you know that, right? I told Raul all about it. He was so proud of you."

As soon as the man mentioned Mr. Ramirez, Lupe knew exactly who was speaking. It was Roberto Clemente, the spirit who appeared when you least expected him. Now he sat in a chair by her bed.

"I cracked up at the plate like that once. Except it was me running home and plowing into the other player," Roberto continued.

"You can remember all that? What are you doing here now?" Lupe asked.

"A player never forgets, Lupe. I figured we had some things to catch up on before I took off," Roberto said.

"What things? Where are you going?" Lupe could picture him clearly in his Pirates jacket. "You're not going to leave Mr. Ramirez, are you?"

"You haven't been by to visit him in a long time. We've noticed." Roberto leaned forward in his chair.

"I know, but I've been busy, playing and coaching, and now look at me." Lupe squirmed under her bed covers.

"I think you've also been busy spending time with Carlos Andrade." Roberto mentioned the one thing Lupe hoped he didn't know about. "Has he come to visit since the accident?"

"The doctor said no visitors, just rest for three days." Lupe wanted to justify Carlos's absence. "You're my first visitor."

"No phone calls, no flowers, nothing?" Roberto wouldn't let his question go unanswered.

"Look around; I've got flowers and cards. Even the kids drew me pictures." Lupe pointed to the dresser full of well wishes. "How is he? Do you know?"

"As a matter of fact, at this very moment he is at a funeral, in Mexico." Roberto was looking at his watch.

"What happened? Who died?" Lupe's heart raced. "Is Celina okay? Is she with him?"

"She is. And her mother and brother are standing next to Carlos." Roberto looked toward the ceiling as if he were imagining the scene. "If I could read his mind, I'd say he is miserable, anxious, and excited all at the same time. Señor Fuentes, his father-in-law, died, and all the Fuentes Coffee workers are at the funeral, too, sizing up Carlos. He has been put in charge of one of the biggest businesses in Mexico."

"So he's staying? He's not coming back?" Lupe wanted to burst into tears but didn't want Roberto to see how much she cared.

"That's part of his misery. Right or wrong, he did love you, Lupe." Roberto nodded his head. "Life is complicated, especially when you are young."

"That's just what Mama said." Lupe recalled her kitchen conversation with her mother. "She said you told her some things about her past, too. If you know all this stuff, why did you ever get on that plane?" Lupe thought of his horrible death that cut his life and career short.

"I did what I thought was right." Roberto straightened his shoulders. "I couldn't see everything before I died. None of us do."

"But what if Mr. Ramirez had never recruited you . . ." Lupe kept talking until she realized that Roberto was no longer sitting in the chair next to her.

"It's about time, slugger," someone said.

"Even with my eyes closed, I know it's you." Lupe rolled her head to the side to see Amelia sitting by her bedside.

"Hey, sleepyhead. They said we couldn't visit you for three days." Amelia shuffled through a stack of crayon drawings the little sluggers delivered to Lupe. "This one says, 'Sorry for the ouchy, Coach Lupe.' That's a keeper."

"Thanks for coming. Don't we have a game today?" Lupe's eyes were wide open. "Have I got my days mixed up? I've been so out of it."

"You're right. I'm headed to the locker room but wanted to see you first." Amelia reached out and touched Lupe's arm. "How you doing?"

"It's weird and boring. I can't wait to get out of this bed." Lupe tried to prop herself up. "I just had the weirdest dream. It was Roberto Clemente again." Lupe tried to remember how much Amelia knew about Roberto. Penny had known the whole story of his appearance, but had she shared it with Amelia?

"Clemente, eh? Was he in a Pirates uniform?" Amelia said.

"Yeah, the jacket. He was talking to me about Carlos Andrade, of all people." As Lupe said this, she realized she had never heard what Carlos and Amelia had talked about at the last East Side Field game.

"Was he? Are you still taking pain pills?" Amelia sat up straight.

"Wait a minute, I remember something, you never told me what you and Carlos talked about at the kid's game. I saw you talking for the longest time, then after the game you both disappeared." Lupe's memory was coming back to her: the win and the sweet revenge against Betty Brewer.

"We'll talk later. It's game time." Amelia gave a little wave and left.

CHAPTER 33

"Can you push me to the kitchen and open the back door?" Lupe looked over her shoulder toward David. "I just want to see Shelly."

"We've got to leave soon if you want to catch part of the game." David gently put his hands on the back of Lupe's chair. "Shelly's probably buried in the sand, anyway."

"She can still hear me." Lupe tried to remember the last time she'd seen her tortoise. "I haven't been out since." Her voice trailed off, remembering the scene Carlos made when he saw Celina reaching into Shelly's box. Whatever made her think he was such a wonderful father?

"Here you go." David opened the back door. "I'm going to make room in the trunk for your chair. I won't be long."

"Shelly," Lupe called out, and she found that her voice was weepy. "Shelly, it's me. I'm sorry I haven't been to see you lately." Lupe could see the bump of her tortoise's shell in the sandbox. "I'm sorry about a lot of things." Lupe felt a dry lump in her throat. "You know I always wanted to do the right thing, to make Mama proud and be a star ballplayer. Now look at me. I'm no good for anyone, not even you." Lupe heard David clearing out the car's trunk in the garage.

"I can't come and feed you now. I can't even feed myself. I'm stuck in this chair." Lupe heard the car trunk slam close. "I'm so sorry." She heard the car engine start and knew she was running out of time. Beyond the bump in the sand, Shelly's head popped up and turned slowly toward Lupe's voice. "You heard me. You understand? I don't know what's going to happen next. I'll make sure someone takes care of you." Lupe leaned forward in her chair, desperate to make contact with her silent pet.

"Okay, you ready?" David turned Lupe's chair toward the makeshift ramp he'd rigged up by the back door. "Hey, she did hear you. I haven't seen her head in ages."

David wheeled Lupe's wheelchair down the ramp at City College to the stadium where her team warmed up for their last game. The girls broke rank and gathered around her, Coach Ferguson standing by her side. Lupe could feel her eyes fill with tears, something she had promised herself that she would not do. She spotted Amelia among the players, and her eyes were misty as well.

"Welcome back," the other players called out. "It's great to see you." For Lupe, their response was heartwarming and heartbreaking at the same time.

Amelia leaned over her to whisper in her ear. "How long?" she asked.

Lupe could only press her lips together and shake her head. She didn't know how much longer she would be in a cast and have to use the wheelchair. Both girls knew that the university coach was not happy to get the news about Lupe's injury.

The umpire signaled for the game to begin, and the players left Lupe's side and headed for the dugout. Her eyes followed them, and she wished she could rise up and go with them.

"Will you be okay alone here until midgame?" David was due at the East Side Field to coach his youth team. That was another place Lupe wished she could go. Her young players had sent homemade get well cards to her, and some of their parents had visited Mama with gifts of food and flowers planted in coffee cans.

"Yeah, fine. I may nod off a little." Lupe shifted an inch in her chair.

"Just don't try to move the chair by yourself." David headed back up the ramp to his car.

"Is this seat taken?" Someone, a woman, approached behind Lupe.

"Ah, no." As she moved into Lupe's line of sight, she recognized the university coach, and her heart began to beat faster. "Coach Shelton! Hi."

"How are you doing, Lupe? Was that your boyfriend?"

"No, my brother, David. He coaches the youth team at the East Side Field." Lupe was proud to say so.

"Baseball runs in the family, eh? I wish more of our players had that kind of support." The coach's words, "our players," hung in the air. Lupe wanted to reach out and clutch them to her chest. Could she be on the team after her recovery? Would her scholarship cover her first year at the university, even if she couldn't play the entire season? She looked back at Coach Shelton but could not bring herself to ask these questions.

"So what do you predict for today's game? Your team has been missing your pitching." The coach looked away from Lupe and out over the field. Lupe wondered if she would be able to pitch as well—or at all—if her leg didn't heal completely or correctly.

"But they've still been winning. I predict it will be the same today. I just wish I could predict my own future." Lupe hinted at her questions.

"Me, too, Lupe, me, too." Lupe could see Amelia watching from her position at shortstop. She wasn't smiling.

CHAPTER 34

By the last inning Lupe was ready to get out of her wheelchair and lie down for a rest. David returned, as promised. Coach Shelton was gone, having said nothing after their initial conversation. The team was well ahead on the scoreboard, but Lupe was tired and depressed to be out of the game and uncertain about her future.

"We've got a quick stop to make before I get you home, sis." He carefully maneuvered her chair up the ramp. "It won't take long; something Mama wanted me to drop off to her at the Villa."

"Before the accident Mama told me something weird about Papa." Lupe studied David's face to see if she ought to share the family secret. "Did you know he was engaged to his old girlfriend in Mexico when he and Mama met?"

"Yeah, the one who wrote to Mama" David said.

"What? She didn't say anything about that." Lupe's heart thudded.

"It turned out she tried to keep him from leaving Mexico." David turned his face toward Lupe. "Some things never change. I think Papa told me as a warning when I was starting high school."

"What if he had gone back to Mexico? What would have happened then?" Lupe asked.

"Well, we wouldn't be around to worry about it, would we?" David gave her another glance. "Is it Mama and Papa we are talking about, or someone else?"

"Of course we're talking about them. Here's something I bet you did not know: when you were in high school, Mr. Ramirez came here to scout you for Major League Baseball." Lupe felt some satisfaction dumping that surprise on David. "He told Mama."

"Now I know you are nuts. Mama didn't tell you that, did she?" He turned the Chevy toward the parking lot at the Villa.

"Do we have to do this now?" This was her first outing in the chair, and she knew she could not face the residents at the Villa, especially Mr. Ramirez. Either her brother did not hear her or chose to ignore her plea. David jerked the car into a parking spot.

The underground parking lot was where Mama used to do the midnight laundry shift. Those days seemed so long ago, but Lupe remembered the look and the smell of the place.

"Why are you getting my chair out?" David didn't answer her but opened the car door. "I'm not kidding; I really can't go in there. Look at me. My life's a wreck."

"You'll be okay. Don't get moody on me." David reached in to lift her out of the car.

"I'm in a horrible mood, and you are right—some of this is about Carlos. I haven't heard from him since the accident." Lupe's words caught in her throat. "The night I was with him, he told me about a game he and Celina play—What If, they call it."

"What night are you talking about?" David was interested.

"Like, what if Papa had not died of a heart attack? Or what if Mama never had to go to work at Villa Santa Barbara?" Lupe whispered her words.

"It happened, Lupe. We'll get over it, just like your leg—it will heal in time," David said.

"What if you had never been arrested?" Lupe lifted her face to her brother. "And what if Carlos never married the girl from Mexico, or had kids, or brought them to the East Side Field?"

"But he did, and there's no changing that." David pulled her arms to help her up.

"You see what a mess I've made of everything?" Lupe was limp. She didn't care about going in. What else would go wrong?

"Here, hold this for me." He removed a large flat box from the back seat and began to roll her wheelchair toward the door. Inside, something was different. The low calm music was piped over the speakers. The dining room was empty. Lupe thought she heard some high-pitched voices, children's voices, which were seldom present at the Villa.

Lupe remembered the first time she had been in the dining room at the Villa. What if she had never come to Villa Santa Barbara to do community service hours? What if Lupe had never spoken Spanish to Mr. Ramirez?

As soon as they turned toward the large theater room where most activities and classes were held, she saw it was full.

"What's this?" Lupe whispered to David. The kids from her little sluggers' team rushed toward her, cheering and calling her name. Their parents stood around the perimeter of the large room. She made a quick scan of the room but did not see Carlos or Celina.

"He's not here, Lupe." Amelia stepped close to her chair and took Lupe's hand.

"I know, but I was still hoping." Lupe smiled at the kids but fought off tears. She spoke in low tones to Amelia. "What did he tell you when you talked at that game?" Amelia bent close to Lupe and whispered in her ear.

"I told him he shouldn't be messing around with you if he didn't really care. He said he did care but there was nothing he could do," Amelia said. "I didn't really understand what he meant then, but now . . ."

The regular Villa residents sat in the middle of the room, many in wheelchairs and walkers. They were all watching Lupe as David rolled her in. In the middle of it all was Mr. Ramirez, with Mama at his side. Everyone clapped and cheered.

"Don't crush the cake!" Mama lifted the box from Lupe's lap, giving her a wink as she bent forward. "Welcome, honey. Listen, everyone is here, cheering for you."

"Cake! Cake!" The children cried out. The residents laughed at their enthusiasm, and the Villa's chef appeared in her high hat to prepare the cake for serving.

Lupe was tearful, and the crowd assumed they were tears of joy because so many people gave her attention and called out her name. She smiled and nodded at everyone. It looked as if she was the most important person in the world. When David rolled her wheelchair into the center of the room, she had an unexpected experience.

She was face-to-face with Mr. Ramirez, who also had tears in his eyes. They were both seated, both being attended by someone behind their wheelchairs, at eye level, looking directly at one another. At this level he looked different. His face was familiar, like an old friend, even a grandpa, but she could also see that he was an old, sick man. When Lupe looked up, she saw it was Roberto Clemente behind Mr. Ramirez's chair. His mouth formed the word *Adios*.

"Lupe, *mi amiga*." Mr. Ramirez's words drew her eyes away from Roberto's face. *"Lo siento, lo siento,"* he repeated as he pointed to her leg.

Their exchange was interrupted when one of the kids brought them both cake. Other residents, including the ladies who played Rummikub and the staff who cared for the residents—all approached one by one to give her greetings, and many remarked about how much Mr. Ramirez had missed her visits. They also looked different from her position in the wheelchair. Some even stood above her, and she soon realized how difficult it was to constantly have to look up to speak to people.

"Thank you, everyone," Lupe kept repeating. Her cake sat untouched in her lap.

"Lupe, look at how loved you are. Today you have made us proud. *Tenemos orgullo.*"

"I didn't do anything, Mama."

"No, *mija*, look at everyone here. You shared yourself, your love, when you had nothing else to share. It is the most precious gift we have to give."

EPILOGUE

Santa Barbara Sporting News

A Roll Call from Our Local Teams

Fall 1996

Lopez Granted Ramirez Legacy Scholarship

A memorial celebration for the life of a little-known MLB recruiter took place at the University Sports Pavilion this week. Former Latin American recruiter Raul Ramirez was honored for his scouting, training, and recruitment of nearly one quarter of Major League Baseball's Latino players over the last fifty years.

Ramirez's final gift to the sport was the endowment of the Ramirez Legacy Scholarship to the University of California at Santa Barbara. At the direction of his final wishes, one female and one male player of Latin American heritage will be awarded full scholarships each year, along with their participation in the softball/ baseball athletic programs.

During an engaging ceremony, the crowd was especially moved to see the former SBCC pitcher and East Side Kids' coach Lupe Lopez rise from her wheelchair to receive the first Ramirez Legacy Scholarship granted by the University.

"Mr. Ramirez and his friends taught me how sports, love, and life go together. For softball, I guess you could say they go hand-in-glove. I owe Mr. Ramirez and my family a lot. I want to play my best, live my best, and make them all proud," Lupe Lopez said.

COMING NEXT

LUPE CROSSES THE LINE, BOOK II

Lupe was eager to get back on the softball field, but regrettably, that would be out of the question. Her team duffle lay abandoned in the recesses of her workplace, untouched, following a triumph three thousand miles away, at a college softball tournament in Massachusetts. Yesterday's heavy downpour flooded the field and in the midst of it all, she faced a new opponent at the University budget meeting. He was the football coach, Derek Unger, who had a deep aversion towards women and wanted her job as Athletic Director at Long Beach State University. She was unprepared for the rivalry she had confronted since she crossed the line from player to coach.

Why did she consistently have to prove herself? After Lupe's impressive performance as a pitcher earned her university recognition, she was a repeat MVP award winner and chosen for multiple All-Star teams. She even worked the mound as a pitcher for the U.S. Olympic Team. Her accomplishments propelled her into a coaching role for a college team, and the Director of the entire Athletic Department. She ultimately hoped to exceed the professional record set by her idol Lisa Fernandez who had coached at UCLA. Derek Unger circulated ugly rumors about her while she was at the Massachusetts tournament with her talented squad.

"Coach, do you need some help here?" Bonnie Gomez, her team center fielder and her summer intern, took good care of Lupe. "You can't do all his by yourself."

"Thanks, Bonnie, but this is my job."

"Aren't you the coach who tells us to work as a team?" Bonnie would not give up.

"Don't worry, I can handle it."

Lupe's old glove, which brought back memories of happier days, lay on her cluttered desk that was piled high with papers. It was too out of reach for her to touch. The start of her financial conference was only thirty minutes away. She had to respond to texts from upset parents and had a voice message from her mom awaiting her reply. She needed to establish a drainage and repair spending allocation for the flooded infield, one that did not impact scholarships, equipment, or travel funds for her championship team, the Long Beach Waves. Another predicament was brewing fifteen hundred miles south of Lupe's Long Beach campus, an issue that would threaten to impact the next decade of her life.

Mexico's Monterrey Sultans made their way to the stadium, and the fans went wild. Cheering from the box, just above the Fuentes Coffee banner, a young woman and her father concentrated on one athlete, Jacob Fuentes Andrade, the center fielder. Jacob had an American style of conducting himself on the field. He was an intense observer with lightning reflexes and a powerful right arm. Not a heckler, not a relaxed goof-off, even when the game was at a sluggish pace, he played like his childhood coach, David Lopez, instructed him in his early years in the States. Teammates referred to him by his American name, Jake. His father, Carlos, and younger sister, Celina, showed up to every game, although the girl wished she could be the one playing for the Sultans.

"Look at that sloppy left fielder, Moreno. He's never learned to hustle out to his position. *Hay que tonto*." Carlos criticized any player who appeared lackadaisical or lazy. He called out the players from the stands and in private to their manager. He felt he had a right to his viewpoints as one of the team's big boosters.

Celina had a different perspective of Moreno, and she had intimate knowledge of his moves off the field. He was one of the team members she would miss when she was accepted to a U.S. college and allowed to further her own softball career.

"*Calmate*, Dad." Celina knew her father was unaware of her secret meetings with the left fielder. That relationship would be over when she secured her admission to Long Beach State University in California. *What was causing the delay of that letter?* She was going to need some time to convince her mother and father to permit her to move back to California before Fall. No need to disturb the waters before she had the college invitation in hand. For twelve years, her education had been guided by the Sisters of Perpetual Suffering. The women of the order had lived up to their name. Celina longed for the carefree childhood she reminisced about in the states. And she longed for the freedom to play ball on her own terms, to use her strength and wit without being confined by the overbearing rules of modesty the nuns, and her parents, expected from her.

ACKNOWLEDGMENTS

My family and friends have been of great
support to me in the writing of
this first book in the Lupe Throws Like A Girl series
and I thank them.
I give special thanks to my new family and friends made up of
fellow writers, including my original
NaNoWriMo Accountability Group
and the professional organizations that have provided
instruction and guidance in the writing
and publishing process, including
the Society for Children's Book Writers and Illustrators
and
the Independent Book Publishers Association.
I cannot say enough about the valuable help
of the publishing professionals at
Bublish Services/Empowering
Authorpreneurs, my hybrid publisher,
and their team of specialists at Bublish.com.
Thank you all.
Let us create many books collaboratively and
connect with countless new readers.

Other Books by Anita Perez Ferguson

The Mission Bells Trilogy

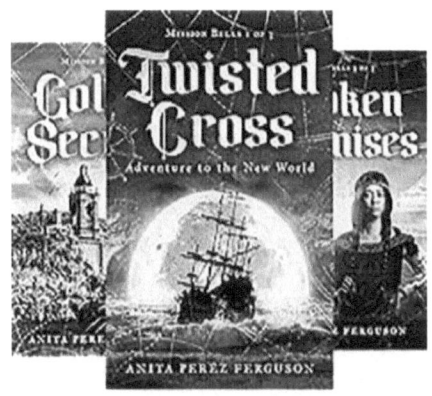

**Twisted Cross, Golden Secrets,
Broken Promises**

Follow and Purchase Anita's books at and all major outlets and
Bublish - Indie Book Publishing & Marketing

See more at:
https://anitaperezferguson.com
https://anitaperezferguson.substack.com